SECRETS AND SORCERY

By Ellie Boswell

THE WITCH OF TURLINGHAM ACADEMY
UNDERCOVER MAGIC
SECRETS AND SORCERY

THE WITCH OF TURLINGHAM ACADEMY

SECRETS AND SORCERY

ELLIE BOSWELL

www.atombooks.net/tween

ATOM

First published in Great Britain in 2012 by Atom

Copyright © 2012 by Working Partners

The moral right of the author has been asserted.

A CIP catalogue record for this book
is available from the British Library.

ISBN 978-1-907410-97-0

Typeset in Minion by M Rules
Printed and bound in Great Britain by
Clays Ltd, St Ives plc

Papers used by Atom are from well-managed forests
and other responsible sources.

MIX
Paper from
responsible sources
FSC® C104740

Atom
An imprint of
Little, Brown Book Group
100 Victoria Embankment
London EC4Y 0DY

An Hachette UK Company
www.hachette.co.uk

www.atombooks.net/tween

With special thanks to Leila Rasheed

PROLOGUE

The wind roared in from the sea and tore across the gardens of Bowden Psychiatric Hospital. Rain rattled against the windows but, inside, Loveday Poulter slept on, her wrinkled face peaceful. There were many shadows in her room, and she did not wake when one of them moved.

The woman who stepped out of the shadows was tall and thin, her hair – tamed only by a jade-lizard hairslide – as wild as one of the trees that tossed outside in the gale. At her heels prowled a Siamese cat, close as a second shadow. The cat miaouled and looked up at her.

'Hush, Mincing,' murmured the woman, with a wary glance towards the door.

A black velvet pouch hung at her side. Out of it, she drew a heavy necklace made of polished stone beads. It seemed to glow with a dull, poisonous, grey tinge, even though there was no light to catch it.

Deep inside, the woman knew she was not quite sane, but she no longer cared. Power was better than sanity. Finally, it was time for revenge on the woman who had separated her from her beloved Robert and ruined her life: her own mother.

Loveday frowned a little, and sighed in her sleep. Her eyelids flickered and her eyes opened. She sat up in bed, blinking sleepily, looking around the dark room. Turning towards the window, she looked straight into her daughter's eyes. A smile broke across her face. 'Oh, Gertrude,' she said. 'My darling girl . . .'

The woman flinched and almost dropped the necklace. Mincing hissed, fur bristling on her arched back.

'Never call me that name!' the woman spat at her

mother. 'Gertrude is dead. I am Angelica now!' She held up the necklace so that her mother could see it. 'Blood and bone, turn to stone . . .'

Her mother's smile disappeared, to be replaced by a look of terror. She reached to pull back the bedclothes, but Angelica moved faster. She flung the necklace towards her mother like a lasso. It fell around her neck, the beads clacking together like teeth.

Angelica grinned as she felt power roar through her, wild as the wind in the trees. 'Blood and bone,' she chanted aloud, 'turn to stone. Cold and old and still as earth, I curse the one who gave me birth!'

Loveday's eyes were wide and frightened as, like a clockwork toy running down, she became completely still. The necklace slowly grew transparent, until it vanished altogether.

Angelica smiled. In the bed, her mother sat like a statue. Only the old woman's eyes moved to follow her daughter as she went to the window and opened it.

A hoarse cry suddenly tore the air. Angelica jumped and spun around to see black wings swooping

3

towards her. She ducked, cursing herself for forgetting about Corvis, her mother's familiar.

The raven pecked at her, beating its wings around her head. Angelica stifled a scream of rage and batted him. She made contact and he landed on the bed, whereupon Mincing pounced.

Corvis took off just too late. He squawked as the cat caught him, biting into his wing, and they fell to the ground as feathers spiralled down.

'Good work, Mincing! Hold him!'

The raven squawked and struggled but the cat kept Corvis pinned down with her claws.

Angelica smiled at her mother in triumph. 'You'll never stop me now,' she hissed. 'This is only the beginning of my vengeance! The rest is soon to come . . . '

To her shock, Angelica saw her mother's lips were moving. She flinched. Her mother had been demagicked long ago; surely she wasn't trying to cast a counter spell? But, no, she was just trying to speak.

'*I love you.*'

Angelica jerked back. For a second her heart ached with a feeling that she thought she had forgotten. But she had buried love with her old name and her old life. She hurried to the window and climbed out.

Mincing let Corvis go with a last hiss and swipe of her claws, and followed her mistress out into the darkness.

ONE

The whole of Turlingham Academy buzzed with the noise of five hundred boarders filing in for assembly. Sophie went in with them, scanning the rows of girls and boys in red and grey for Katy. Monday morning was always about swapping the weekend's gossip, but this Monday morning's gossip was off the scale! There was all the stuff with her Aunt Angelica, and Sophie's dad coming back from out of the blue. Sophie had hardly slept all night – every time she had closed her eyes she had woken up again, remembering the magic orbs flying through the air; her aunt's face, twisted with anger; and then the door flying open and her father striding in to rescue her and Katy. At least it was all over now, and her aunt gone for good.

And yet she couldn't feel truly happy. Katy was the only person she could talk to because she was the only person who knew the truth about everything. But, as a witch and a witch hunter, their friendship was never going to be straightforward.

She grinned as she saw Katy sitting cross-legged on the floor among the other Year 9s. Katy spotted her at the same moment and waved. Sophie edged along the row and squeezed in next to her best friend.

'Hey, Sophie!' Erin's loud American accent greeted her from the row behind. Beside Erin, Lauren beamed. From the row in front, Kaz and Joanna leaned back to say hi.

'Hi, guys,' Sophie said to her friends, and shot a warning glance at Katy. They couldn't talk magic in front of the others.

'Hey, Sophie, how are you?' Katy asked. 'How did it

go with your mum and dad? I bet she was shocked to see him.'

'Um, yeah, just a bit.' Sophie laughed, settling herself on the parquet floor.

Her stomach churned when she thought about her father being home. She knew things were going to be complicated: he'd been gone for ten years and her mum wasn't going to forgive him overnight. Even though Sophie knew that her dad had to leave, to keep her and her mum safe from witch hunters, he hadn't told her mum the truth. Sophie wanted things to work out so much, but how could it when there were so many secrets?

'But you're the one with the real gossip,' she said, changing the subject to safer ground. 'What happened between you and Callum last night, then, eh?'

'Oh, yes! Give us the deets!' Erin scooched further forwards while Joanna and Kaz and Lauren leaned over eagerly.

Katy blushed. 'Well, I, um, he . . . er—' She glanced at Kaz.

Sophie cringed, suddenly remembering that Kaz

had a big crush on Callum. To her relief, Kaz shook her curly hair and laughed out loud.

'Oh, don't worry, Katy. I'm *so* over that. You two were meant for each other – and, anyway, I'm interested in someone else now.'

'No way!' Erin's mouth fell open. 'Who? When? How?'

'Oliver.' Kaz beamed as everyone's attention turned to her. 'We hung out at the parade last night.'

Erin squealed, and the girls all started asking questions at once.

'Are you proper boyfriend and girlfriend? Did he ask you out?' Lauren asked, wide-eyed.

'Not exactly, but I know if we had a bit more time together he would!' Kaz turned to Katy. 'What about you? Did Callum ask you out last night?'

'Yeah, put us out of our misery, Katy, and tell us!' Sophie begged.

'Shhh!' a furious voice hissed from behind them. Sophie jumped and looked around. Maggie Millar – the head prefect – frowned at them and nodded to the front of the hall.

Sophie and her friends turned round as Sophie's mother stepped onto the stage, wearing her most headmistressy expression. Sophie sighed: Katy's gossip would have to wait.

'Good morning, Turlingham.' Her mother's voice was hoarse and she had bags under her eyes. Sophie hoped no one else could tell how tired she was. The room fell silent: the youngest boarders gaping up at the headmistress, and the teachers and prefects at the back of the room gently shushing the older girls.

'I have some very exciting news for you today,' Sophie's mum went on. 'As you may remember, every two years the Year 9s and 10s have the option of taking part in the Earl of Turlingham Gold Award.'

Sophie sat up straight and exchanged glances with her friends.

'The award offers you the chance to get involved in our local community in a variety of exciting ways. It's hard work and it means giving up several hours of your free time, but it will look excellent on your school record and help with university applications when the time comes – although I know that seems very far away to most of you.' Sophie's mum smiled. 'Some Year 11s will also be needed as volunteers to assist Mrs Freeman.'

Sophie didn't mean to groan, but she couldn't help it. The rest of her year did the same. Mrs Freeman was the girls' housemistress, and she was terrifying!

Sophie's mum smiled at Mrs Freeman.

'After assembly you can sign up for your chosen activity on the lists on your year's notice-board,' she went on. 'There are two levels to the award: Silver and Gold. Once students have completed the Silver Award to Mrs Freeman's satisfaction, they will be allowed to proceed to the Gold Award – an expedition to Holland!'

An excited murmur ran around the hall. Joanna and Kaz nodded at each other, and Sophie heard Erin whisper to Lauren, 'Oh, wow, that means I get to go on holiday with Mark . . . Super cool!'

Katy nudged Sophie, and Sophie grinned back. She totally agreed with Erin – they'd sign up as soon as assembly was over!

Sophie headed for the doors as soon as the prefects opened them, eager to get to the sign-up sheets before the activities filled up. But it seemed as if everyone else in Year 9 and 10 had had the same idea! Sophie dodged a big boy's bag and followed Erin and Kaz as they wove in and out of the crowd hurrying in the direction of the notice-boards.

'No running in the corridors!' Maggie called after them. 'Sophie Morrow, that means you!'

Sophie rolled her eyes. Why did Maggie always pick on her? She forced herself to walk – at least until Maggie was out of sight. Then she and her friends raced down the flagstone corridor after everyone else, but skidded to a halt when they reached the edge of the crowd in front of the boards.

Sophie jumped on tiptoes, trying to see the lists of activities. A tall girl flicked her ponytail in Sophie's face and shoved past her.

'It's impossible. I can't even see what the activities are, let alone get near enough to put my name down,' Sophie reported back to her friends.

Finally the crowd thinned enough so that Sophie was able to get to the front.

'OK – so these are the options,' she called back to

her friends, then read out: 'Organising a jumble sale. Running in the Turlingham Village Sponsored Run. Helping with the sixth formers' charity fashion show—'

'Oh, cool!' Erin's eyes shone.

'—reading with primary school children. Helping at a soup kitchen. Working on a farm. Assisting the school librarian—'

Sophie and Katy exchanged a glance, remembering the adventures they'd had in the school library just a few weeks ago. They were the only people who knew it had a magic side!

'—litter-picking in the village. Helping at Seaview Dogs' Home and ... I think that's all of them.' She struggled out of the crowd again and joined the others.

'Oh, I can't decide!' groaned Lauren. 'They all sound like fun.'

'Me neither,' said Sophie. 'Katy, what do you want to do?'

'What about Seaview Dogs' Home?' Katy suggested. 'The puppies there are sooo cute.'

'Hey, guys!' A boy's voice broke in and Sophie looked up to see Callum Pearce, tall and thin with his curly hair sticking out, his glasses slightly askew and his shirt untucked, striding towards them. She stifled a smile – he might be the headmaster's son, but he definitely didn't look the part!

'Hi, Callum,' said Katy. 'We can't decide what activities to do.'

Callum squinted at the list. 'I thought maybe the Village Run, but I don't know.'

'That sounds good, doesn't it, Sophie?' Katy said eagerly.

Sophie grinned. Katy was no runner but Sophie knew she would want to do whatever Callum was doing. 'OK, let's have a look.' She got out her pen and pushed her way back through the thinning crowd. As she examined the board she saw another list, right at the edge. It was headed: *The Bowden Psychiatric Hospital Vegetable Garden Project.*

'Oh, look!' she exclaimed. Her granny was in the Bowden hospital – some years ago, she had tried to tell people of the existence of witches and witch hunters in their world, and had been 'put somewhere safe' for her pains – and, she realised, as she felt her squirrel familiar move in her bag, running around a garden would be perfect for Gally!

Katy and Callum came over. Sophie pointed to the sign.

'It's only one Saturday, too – the others are eight hours spread over two weeks,' she said. 'So it would be one day of really hard work, but then we'd have the Silver award!'

'Perfect,' Katy agreed. 'What do you think, Callum?'

'Sounds good to me!' Callum took his pen and wrote their three names.

As Sophie turned around, she saw that Erin and Mark were standing behind them. Erin had her arms folded, and Mark looked annoyed.

'You're nuts! A sponsored run?' Erin was saying. 'Come on, Mark, can you imagine me in sweats?'

'Oh, just because I don't want to put on a fashion show!' Mark said. 'What's nuts about wanting to get outdoors and do stuff?'

'Why don't you both come and do the gardening with us?' Sophie suggested, hurrying up to them.

'Have you signed up for that?' Erin studied the notice-board. 'What do you think, Mark? Could you go for gardening?'

Mark shrugged. 'I suppose.'

Erin signed them up and smiled at Sophie. 'Thanks, Sophie!' She glanced around but Mark was already disappearing down the corridor. 'Hey, Mark – wait!' She ran off after him.

Katy caught Sophie's eye. 'World War Three averted . . . for now!' she whispered.

Sophie grinned.

'Um, Katy,' said Callum, clearing his throat. 'Could I walk you to your first lesson?'

Katy blushed. 'Of course.'

'Er . . . I'll stay here for a bit,' said Sophie, hanging back. She wondered if Callum would ever get round to asking Katy out – surely all her efforts to get them together couldn't be for nothing. It was so obvious they really liked each other!

She turned back to the board and saw a tall,

dark-haired, green-eyed boy studying her with a look of amusement. Ashton Gibson: Katy's brother, and Sophie's biggest headache.

Ashton put his hands in his pockets and examined the lists. His eyes glittered under his fringe.

'Hmm, lots to choose from. What have you signed up for, Sophie?'

Sophie took a deep breath. She didn't want Ashton in her group for the award: she needed to keep as far away from him as possible. He was a witch hunter, and that meant whenever he was around, Sophie was in danger.

'None of your business,' she said, wishing it didn't make her sound quite so childish.

Ashton just grinned, and Sophie bit her lip.

'Yeah, there's a lot of choice,' Ashton went on. 'Activities to suit all kinds of people. Now if I were a witch, for example, what would I choose?' He turned to her. 'Sophie?'

Sophie folded her arms. *Here we go*, she thought.

'Not being a witch, Ashton,' she said, as calmly as she could, 'I wouldn't know.'

Ashton gave a triumphant yell. 'Aha – vegetable gardening!' He placed his finger on her scribbled name. 'Do you know, I've always dreamed of digging up a carrot or two. Finally, I get my chance.' He caught Sophie's eye and, despite her annoyance, she had to laugh. She couldn't imagine anyone less likely to be into gardening than Ashton, and he knew it.

Ashton pulled out his silver fountain pen and signed his name on the list with a flourish. Sophie waited until he had finished.

'You know what?' she said brightly. 'I don't think I'm that into gardening, after all. It seems to attract the wrong crowd.' She crossed out her name and wrote it down on the next list.

'Oh, right, I see.' Ashton put a line through his own name and wrote it beneath hers. '*Obviously* training to run the Turlingham Village Run is so much more your style.' Sophie's face fell as she realised what she'd signed up for. 'So long as you don't use your broomstick,' he added, with a grin. 'That would be cheating.'

'You're so out of date, Ashton. Don't you know all the best witches ride vacuum cleaners these days?'

Sophie snapped back. She crossed out her name and signed herself up for the fashion show – surely Ashton wouldn't be into something that girly? But he was already leaning over her, his pen at the ready. Sophie furiously crossed out her name and added it to the next list.

But whatever Sophie signed up for, Ashton followed her – until she saw she was about to sign her name again underneath one of her crossed-out names.

'Whoops,' she said. The notice-board was a mess. The neat sign-up sheets were crumpled and creased, and covered in crossings-out.

This is not a good time to laugh, she thought – but then she caught Ashton's eye. He was biting back a grin. Sophie spluttered a giggle, and Ashton burst out laughing at the same moment.

For a split second, Sophie thought that Ashton looked especially cute when he was laughing – then, annoyed with herself, she squashed the thought and frowned at him instead.

She turned back to the board. If Ashton was going

to follow her in whatever she signed up for, she might as well be with her friends.

She wrote her name under the vegetable garden project again, and then stepped back from the notice-board. Ashton signed under her name. He looked at her expectantly. Sophie shook her head.

'You win this time,' she said. 'But just stay away from me, Ashton Gibson, or you'll be sorry!'

She turned on her heel and stalked off to class, wondering how she'd managed to share a laugh with Ashton. It wasn't as if she needed reasons to dislike him: not only was he horrible, he was determined to denounce her as a witch. Sure, he could be charming, but that was all part of his scheme to get her to drop her guard. There was no way she would let herself fall for those green eyes . . . was there?

TWO

When the bell rang for the end of Monday's classes, Sophie ran to meet Katy in front of the main doors. She was still dying to talk to her about everything that had happened, but they couldn't risk it until they were well away from everyone else.

They walked quickly away from the crowd, shouts and whistles from the hockey players practising on the field ringing through the air. Beyond the fence, the Turlingham lighthouse towered over them, casting its long shadow out to sea.

Sophie wrapped her coat tightly around her, her feet crunching on dry leaves. As soon as she was sure no one could overhear them, she turned to Katy.

'Are you sure you're OK?' she asked her. 'I was so scared when my aunt flung her evil magic at you – I thought you would be killed!'

'I'm fine, I promise. Thanks to the gold you added to my friendship bracelet!' Katy lifted her wrist and shook her bracelet. Sophie smiled as her gold earrings glinted in among the charms. Gold protected witch hunters against witches – it was a good thing she had found that out before Angelica had attacked Katy.

Blushing slightly, Katy went on: 'Actually, I feel so happy I don't think anything could ever hurt me again!'

'Oh, Katy! Is it . . .?' Katy's blushing, beaming face told Sophie her guess was right. 'It's Callum, isn't it?'

'He asked me to be his girlfriend!' Katy blurted out. 'And I said yes!'

Sophie squealed and jumped up and down.

'Katy! Oh, wow! Last night?'

Katy nodded.

'I'm so happy for you!' Sophie flung her arms around Katy in a hug, then pulled away. 'OK,' she said mock-sternly, 'now you owe me an apology. You and Callum have officially been going out for' – she glanced at her watch – 'nearly twenty-four hours, and I only get to hear *now*!'

'Oh, well . . . ' Katy bit her lip. 'I thought you had enough to deal with last night, what with your dad coming back so suddenly like that.'

Sophie sighed, suddenly feeling deflated. It was so easy to be happy about Callum and Katy getting together that she'd forgotten there was a complicated mess waiting for her at home.

'Your mum must have been pretty shocked, seeing him after so many years,' Katy said. 'How's it going?'

'Well,' Sophie said. 'Mum fainted when she saw him, which is pretty understandable.' Katy nodded. 'And after she came round I left them to talk.' Sophie still hadn't had a chance to speak to either of them to find out how it went. 'The good news is he was still there when I came downstairs this morning.'

'That's positive,' Katy said.

'But the bad news is he stayed on the sofa.'

'Hmm, not so good.'

'Exactly.' Sophie nodded. 'It could go either way.'

They were nearly at her cottage, which stood a little away from the main school building. She swallowed.

'Well, hey, at least this Earl of Turlingham Award looks as if it'll be really good fun!' Katy said, obviously trying to lighten the mood. But then her face fell and she added, 'That is, if my annoying brother doesn't ruin it. I saw he signed up for the vegetable garden, too. Like he's bothered about digging an allotment!' She threw up her hands. 'I'm really sorry he's bugging you so much.'

Sophie did something halfway between a laugh and a sigh. There would always be witch hunters after her. At least Ashton was a known threat – and she reckoned she could handle him.

'Honestly, Katy, you don't have to apologise. It's not your fault your brother's being such a pain!'

Katy laughed.

Sophie glanced around, bent down and unzipped

her bag. Gally poked his sleek black head out, ears and whiskers twitching. He touched his nose to her Source – the crescent-moon ring that she needed to cast spells – and, as she straightened up, he scrambled up her skirt into her coat pocket. Sophie gently stroked his fur and looked up at the cottage.

'Well – time to find out how Mum and Dad are getting on!'

She pushed open the gate and they walked up the path towards the cottage. As Sophie put her key in the door, she hesitated; she was sure she had heard the sound of chuckling from inside. Katy didn't seem to have heard anything yet, but that was normal. Sophie had excellent hearing: all witches did.

She put a finger to her lips and turned the key gently in the lock. She heard the laughter again as she pushed the door open, and this time Katy nodded excitedly at her. They tiptoed to the living-room door, which was shut, and listened.

'. . . and do you remember that camping holiday we took on Jersey?' her father was saying.

'When the cow got into the tent?' Sophie's mother

giggled. 'And you said, "Well, it's a fresh milk delivery!" I'd forgotten how bad your jokes are.'

Sophie had to stop herself from cheering. Laughing together was a sign of love, wasn't it? She beamed at Katy, then tapped Katy's hand in a quiet high five.

'You're as beautiful as the day I married you.' Sophie's father's voice dropped low. Sophie could see from Katy's expression that she couldn't hear them any more. 'Do you remember our wedding day?'

There was a pause.

'Of course,' said her mother. The happiness was gone from her voice. 'I remember us promising to be together for better or worse. But that doesn't seem to have happened, does it?'

'I know.' Her father's voice was so soft that even Sophie had to strain to hear it. 'I'm so sorry, Tamsin.'

'I want it to be a new start, so much. But I can't do that unless you're honest with me.'

Sophie held her breath. *Oh please, Dad,* she thought. *Just tell her the truth.*

After a long pause, her father answered.

'I – I wish I could be. Would you just trust me?'

'How can I?' Her mum's voice rose. 'You won't tell me the truth about where you've been. Ten years, Frank! I raised Sophie alone.'

And I grew up without a dad, thought Sophie. Katy squeezed her hand gently.

'I know. I know. I wish I could explain.' Sophie heard her father pace back and forth. 'Some people were after me. I had to leave for everyone's safety.'

'People?' Sophie's mum's voice squeaked. 'What people? What have you got yourself mixed up in?'

Sophie bit her lip as the silence stretched out. She knew that her father was saying as much as he dared to.

'If you won't tell me, how can I trust you?' Sophie's mum said finally. Her voice was sad, not angry. Eventually, she sighed. 'Listen, I'll let you stay a few days. For Sophie's sake. But if you can't give me a decent answer, then you'll have to leave.'

'Tamsin—'

'I mean it. I'm sorry.'

Sophie and Katy jumped back as the door was pulled open and her mother walked out, still in her work suit. She stopped dead as she saw them.

'Katy! Sophie!' Her face reddened a little. 'Were you listening?'

'I'm sorry!' Sophie burst out. 'I know I shouldn't have listened, but I ... ' She found herself speaking through tears. 'I just want you and Dad to be ... to be ... together.'

Katy put an arm around her shoulders and hugged her.

Her father had come to the door, and was standing behind her mother. Sophie wiped her tears away and looked into his warm brown eyes. More than anything, she didn't want their family to split up again.

'Katy, dear, perhaps ... ' Sophie's mum began.

Katy nodded at once and started backing towards the front door. 'I'll see you at school tomorrow, Sophie,' she said, giving Sophie's hand a last squeeze.

Sophie gave her a wobbly smile as she went out of the door, then turned back to her parents.

'Oh, please, Mum, give him a chance!'

Her mother turned and exchanged a glance with her husband. Together, they moved towards her and hugged her. Sophie felt their warm arms around her and wondered why it couldn't always have been like this. Why it couldn't *stay* like this?

'Sophie,' her dad said gently. 'We love each other very much. But what I did is very hard to forgive. Especially when I'm asking for blind trust.'

There was a warning note in his voice. Sophie hung her head. She knew what he meant. Even if it meant he had to leave, there was no way he would tell her mother the truth about their magic, and risk putting her in danger.

'Yes, look how strong our love is – it made you!' Sophie's mum said, stroking Sophie's hair. 'I don't know if we can work things out. But, whatever happens, both of us love you and always will.'

Sophie looked up. Her mum's eyes were full of tears.

'I need a few moments alone ... I'm sorry,' her mum murmured. She hurried up the stairs, and Sophie heard the bedroom door click shut.

Nothing's easy when you're a witch, Sophie thought. She wished there was a spell that could make everything right.

*

Sophie trudged into the kitchen with her dad. He sat at their table, dangling his gold pocket watch by its chain. Sophie knew it was his Source. It shone in the kitchen lights, and the fox engraved on the casing seemed to grin as the light played on it. He looked up and gave her a tired smile.

'At times like this I wish Rosdet was here,' he said. 'My familiar was such a wonderful, handsome, clever fox. But he's gone now . . . a long time ago.' His voice tailed off and he looked sad.

Sophie felt sorry for him. She couldn't imagine life without Gally. And, after all, it wasn't Dad's fault he couldn't be honest with Mum. She wanted to ask about Rosdet, but she sensed it wasn't the right time.

'Do you want a cup of tea?' she suggested.

'That sounds great,' he answered.

Sophie walked over to the Aga and put the kettle on. As she waited for the water to boil, she gazed out at the wintery back garden. A cat slunk across the garden fence and Sophie shivered – but it was only an ordinary tabby, not a Siamese like Mincing. *Where is Angelica now?* she wondered. She hoped she was far away. Perhaps she had found her husband, Robert Lloyd, again. Love could fix anything. *At least,* she thought, remembering her mum and dad, *I really, really, really hope it can.*

The kettle whistled and she quickly made two cups of tea.

'I'm glad you're back, Dad,' she said, smiling at him as she passed him one of the mugs.

'Me, too,' he said. 'I can't tell you how much I've missed you.'

Sophie curled her legs around the chair. 'Dad ... why not tell Mum the truth? Then she'd understand.'

Her father sighed. 'It's not that simple, Sophie. The less your mother knows, the less danger she's in. Last night, when my sister attacked you ...' He shook his head. 'It just proves how real and unpredictable the danger is. And not only from witch hunters. Angelica doesn't seem to care about loyalty to witches any more, and that scares me. The only thing that matters is keeping you and your mother safe.' He took a sip of his tea and whispered, 'Even if it means I have to be separated from you.'

'But, Dad—'

'Besides, can you imagine what she'd think if I told her that you and I are both witches? If I said I had to leave home to escape witch hunters?' He laughed without humour. 'She'd think we were mad. We'd end up in a place like your grandmother.'

Sophie swallowed. It was hard to admit it to herself, but she knew her father was right.

'I know it's tough, Sophie,' her dad said. He put down his tea and reached out to hold her hand.

Sophie forced a smile.

'Sophie,' he went on, 'I want you to be very careful when you're out and about. I know we drove Gertrude – Angelica, or whatever she calls herself now – away, but she still has her spell book.' He frowned. 'There's a saying that if there's a wasp in the room, it's best to know where it is. I don't know where Angelica is, and that worries me.'

Sophie nodded silently. So Angelica might strike again. The thought was like a cold stone in her stomach. It wasn't over – not yet.

Her father withdrew his hand and drummed his

fingers on the table. 'We have to find her,' he said, as if to himself. 'If I hadn't been there in time last night, she might have killed you.'

Sophie gripped the edge of the table. 'Oh, Dad, do you think so? I mean,' her voice wobbled, 'she's my aunt! She wouldn't really hurt a member of her own family, would she?'

Her father shook his head, looking very serious. 'I don't want to believe it, but she is unhinged.' He stared into his mug. 'It's as if Gertrude, my twin sister, has vanished. All that's left is Angelica, the cruel, angry person that she's chosen to become.'

He looked up and met Sophie's eyes. He gave a brief smile. 'There's still a chance. Perhaps we can persuade her to live peacefully, with her family where she belongs.'

Sophie echoed his smile, but her heart wasn't in it. 'And . . . if we can't?' she replied.

Her father looked down at his mug again, and his hands tightened around it. There was a pause. Sophie took a sip of tea.

'Then,' he said very quietly, 'I will do whatever I have to, to protect my family.'

Sophie wondered why he sounded so serious. She remembered the powerful spell he had used to stop Angelica hurting them last night, the fierce look in his eyes as he had defended her. She knew he didn't want to harm his sister, but if Angelica pushed him too far, what might happen?

She put her tea down; her hand was suddenly shaking so hard that the liquid was spilling out of the mug. She didn't want Angelica to come to harm, no matter how bad she was, and she didn't want her father to do something he would regret, not even to defend her and her mother.

There must be some way we can stop Angelica from being evil, she thought. *This can't happen. Things can't be this horrible – someone must be able to influence her.*

But who? Perhaps Grandma? She was her mother, after all. Or . . . what about Angelica's husband?

'Dad,' she blurted out, 'what about Robert Lloyd?'

Her father looked up. 'What about him?'

'Well, couldn't he persuade Angelica to stop using her magic to harm people? I mean, they love each other so much.' She suddenly felt hopeful. 'That's it!

Angelica's so angry and unhappy because the witch and witch hunter communities drove her and Robert apart. Maybe if we got them back together, she'd be happy, and she'd stop wanting revenge.'

Her father shook his head slowly, his face firm.

'Robert Lloyd is a witch hunter,' he said, as if the answer were obvious. 'I've never met him but I know I don't want him anywhere near my sister. My mother was right to separate them.'

'But, Dad—'

'Listen, Sophie.' His voice was very serious. 'Witch hunters hate us just because of what we are: witches. It doesn't matter if we're bad or good. It isn't enough for them to steal our Sources and stop us from doing magic. No,' his face hardened, 'they have to demagick us, to stop us being witches at all.' His voice shook. 'They don't want us to even exist.'

Sophie was frightened by the expression on his face. She had never seen him look so deeply angry, though he spoke calmly.

'But Katy—' she began timidly.

'I know you and Katy are friends, but ... you are

very young.' He sighed. 'If Katy stays friends with you, she's going to have to make some tough choices.'

Sophie felt tears prick her eyes. Her father leaned over and pressed her hand comfortingly.

'Don't worry,' he said. 'This is for me to sort out, not you.' He smiled. 'Now why don't you tell me how your witchcraft is coming along? I understand that you didn't get your Source' – he glanced at the crescent-moon ring on Sophie's finger – 'until after your thirteenth birthday. That would slow you down a little, I imagine.'

Sophie jumped up, feeling happier at once. 'It's going great! I'll show you.'

She looked around the kitchen for inspiration. On the windowsill was a geranium cutting that her mother was cultivating. Sophie looked around and then picked up a glass from the draining board.

Wondering if her idea would work – she had never tried it before – she rubbed her Source against the glass, and murmured: 'Forces of the Earth, make this plant grow! Earth, water, wind and fire, give it your strength . . .'

She held up the glass so that the last rays of the setting sun shone through the bottom. Sophie looked from the glass to the shoot, worried: maybe the sun wasn't strong enough.

Her Source glowed suddenly, as if the sun was reflecting from it, and Sophie felt warmth coming from the glass in her hand. Her fingers tingled, and the tingling ran up her arms and through her whole body. She shivered. The magic was working!

A green leaf popped out of the geranium cutting, and then another. Sophie whooped with excitement. Her father pushed back his chair and hurried over to see.

'Well done, Sophie!' he exclaimed, as the cutting swelled into a green, bushy plant covered with bright red flowers. 'Though maybe you'd better stop now.'

Sophie jumped back as the geranium plant's roots suddenly shot across the draining board and down the plughole. Her father grabbed the glass and the geranium stopped growing.

'Wow!' Sophie stared at what her magic had done. 'I've never—'

The phone rang in the hallway. From upstairs, Sophie heard her mother call, 'I'll get it!'

'Very impressive!' Sophie's dad said, stroking her hair. 'But we'd better get it outside before the roots block the drains!'

They were trying to uproot the geranium when Sophie heard her mum running down the stairs. Sophie exchanged a look with her dad. He wrestled with the geranium and managed to pull it up. Opening the window, he tossed it outside – just as Sophie's mother burst through the door. Her face was pale and her eyes were wide.

'Tamsin? What's the matter?' her father asked.

'It's the hospital,' she said. 'Your mother's not well.'

Sophie's heart turned over.

'Sophie, get your coat.' Her father went to the door. Sophie followed him, her heart thumping. Her grandma was an old woman, and she'd been through a lot recently. *Oh, please let her be OK!* Sophie thought desperately, as they ran to the car.

THREE

The glass doors of Bowden Hospital slid open in front of Sophie and her family as they raced up the stone steps. Sumira, the receptionist, looked up as they came in.

'Oh, Mrs Morrow – I'm so sorry about what has happened.' She came around the desk and squeezed Sophie's mum's hands. Even though Sumira was being sweet, Sophie just wanted to get to her grandma.

'Your mother-in-law seems very calm,' Sumira continued, 'but there has been no change. The doctor is with her now.' She glanced at Sophie's father.

'This is Loveday's son,' said Sophie's mum.

'Oh! Pleased to meet you.' Sumira's voice was cold, and Sophie knew, as she followed her parents through the long corridors, that the receptionist was wondering why he had never come to see his mother before.

Poor Dad, she thought. *No one understands.*

A doctor in a white coat and a turban met them outside Grandma's door.

'Are you her family?' he said gravely as they reached him. 'You must prepare yourself for a shock.'

He pushed the door open and they walked in behind him. Sophie saw a tall, balding man, dressed in a care-assistant's uniform, bending over her grandmother, who was a frail shape lying in the bed.

'Mum!' Her father rushed towards the bed.

Tamsin stopped short. 'Oh my goodness! What's happened to her hair?'

The care assistant looked up quickly. A second later, he had scuttled past them, out of the door, and then all of Sophie's attention was on her grandmother. Her eyes widened as she saw for herself: her grandmother's grey hair had turned bright white. She lay motionless in the bed, a fixed half-smile on her face.

The doctor's face was serious as he studied her chart. 'Mrs Poulter is very ill indeed. Paralysed, it seems. We believe it's a stroke. Although ... ' – he glanced at the bed, and frowned as he went on – 'it's unlike any stroke I've ever seen before. We can't account for the loss of pigmentation in the hair.'

'Is she – is she going to die?' Sophie asked.

The doctor locked eyes with Sophie. 'I'm afraid I just don't know.' He turned to Sophie's parents. 'She's stable, and appears comfortable. But we can't say how long this ... *coma* will last. And if it lasts too long ...' He tailed off. 'We should know more in time.'

Sophie felt a sob welling up inside her. Her poor grandmother – she was always so strong, so kind, and now she was completely helpless and might even die. She burst into tears.

'Oh, Sophie.' Her father put a tender arm around her. Over her head he said to Sophie's mum. 'It's the shock ... could you get Sophie a cup of sweet tea?'

'Of course!' Sophie's mum hugged her too, and then hurried out of the room.

'I'll leave you alone for a few moments,' the doctor said, sounding embarrassed. He made for the door, and soon Sophie and her father were alone.

As soon as they were, Sophie's father shook her gently.

'Sophie!' His voice was urgent, and she was startled into stopping crying. 'It's not an illness. It's a curse – I'm sure of it. This must be the work of a witch hunter.'

Sophie rubbed her eyes.

'Look at her face.' Her father leant over his mother, looking carefully into her eyes. 'There's light in her eyes ... as if she's trapped. But we'll have to find out exactly what kind of curse it is before we can lift it.'

Her father drew out his Source. Sophie felt Gally fidgeting in her coat pocket. As soon as she lifted him out, he jumped onto the bed and sniffed at Grandma, his fur bristling. Suddenly, he stood up on his hind legs, his ears pointing forwards and his nose twitching. Then he leapt over Grandma's body and disappeared off the far side of the bed. Sophie saw him sniffing at something on the carpet. It was a black feather.

'Corvis!' Sophie exclaimed. She hurried round the bed and picked up the feather.

Gally darted here and there, nosing under the furniture, Sophie following him.

'Corvis,' she called. 'Come out ... it's us ... it's safe.'

She knelt down and looked under the bookcase. A bright eye blinked back at her.

'Oh, Corvis,' she gasped as the crow shuffled out, dragging a wing behind him.

Her dad bent to pick him up. 'Find a blanket, Sophie. We'll get him to a vet as soon as we can.'

Sophie hunted around and found a blanket and a shoebox in Grandma's wardrobe. She made a nest for Corvis and her father lifted him in. The crow let out a weak squawk and closed his eyes. Gally stood on his hind legs and looked in, a worried tilt to his ears.

'Don't worry Gally, Corvis will be better soon,' Sophie whispered, stroking the crow's head.

'Sophie, keep an eye on the door,' her father said. He stood up and glanced around. 'I need a sewing needle.'

'Grandma always keeps a sewing kit in her top drawer,' Sophie offered. She went to the bedroom door and listened. She could hear distant footsteps and voices, but no one seemed to be coming their way. Meanwhile, her father opened the drawer and took out the sewing kit. Sophie tensed as a trolley squeaked past in the corridor outside.

Her father pulled a chair up to his mother's bedside and sat down.

'Now, Sophie, this is an important thing for you to see,' he said. 'Pay close attention.'

Sophie winced as her father pressed a sewing needle gently into Grandma's arm and drew it out again. She waited for the blood to appear but, instead, a thin stream of what looked like smoke leaked from the puncture. Soon there was a murky, grey aura hanging around her grandmother's still body.

'What is it, Dad?'

'I'm not sure.' Her father rubbed his chin. 'A witch

hunter process should produce a purple aura, not a grey one like this.'

'But it *is* a curse?' Sophie asked. She touched the grey aura with a finger, and shuddered. It felt as cold and clammy as an old tomb.

'Yes. And now we have to find out who has put it on your grandmother.'

He hung his pocket watch above his mother's eyes and allowed it to swing back and forth on the chain, as if he were hypnotising her.

'Forces of the Earth,' he chanted, 'earth, water, wind and fire. Lend me your sight, water that reflects all things on the earth, wind that blows over everyone, earth that witnesses everything, fire that lights the way in darkness. Show me the secrets locked in her eyes.'

Sophie, filled with awe, leaned forwards to look into her grandmother's eyes. There seemed to be a shape reflected in them: a dark figure. She could feel her own Source tingling as her father's pocket watch swung back and forth, back and forth, gleaming.

'Fetch me a bowl of water,' her father told her. 'The

spell reflects the last thing that she saw before the curse was placed on her.'

Sophie ran to the sink, emptied out the toothbrush mug and filled it with water. She brought it back to her father and he moved the pocket watch carefully over to the water and swung it above it. As he did so, an image slowly formed in the water, as if it were oil on the surface.

It was a woman. Her face, twisted with anger, was framed with wild curly hair in which a green slide shaped like a lizard glinted. She had her hand in the air and she was flinging something forwards: a stone necklace.

'Angelica!' Sophie gasped.

As if it had heard her speak, the image dissolved into nothingness.

'Was it Angelica who did this?' Sophie couldn't believe that anyone would put a curse on their own mother.

'I suspected as much,' her father said, and he clenched his jaw. 'This is strange, powerful magic, like nothing I've ever seen before. I don't think it is witch hunter magic after all.' He frowned deeply. 'And I don't think I can break the curse, at least, not yet.'

Sophie was silent with shock. There was no question about it – Angelica had to be caught and persuaded to break the curse. But she wasn't sure which was more frightening: the fact that her aunt was mad enough to do this to her own mother, or the expression on her father's face when he had seen Angelica's image in the water.

FOUR

Sophie pushed open the door of the common room, and looked around. She sighed in relief as Katy waved to her from the study corner. Dumping her bag on the table, Sophie ran over to her.

'I'm so glad I found you! I've looked all over the school.' The best friends hugged each other. 'We've got to talk.' She pulled away from the hug and glanced around to check that no one was listening, and whispered, 'Angelica's put my grandma under a curse. It's paralysed her.' Katy looked shocked. Sophie quickly described her grandmother's white hair, the grey smoke that had come out of her, and the image that had formed in the water. Katy listened, frowning.

'Your dad's right,' she said, when Sophie had finished. 'Witch hunter processes do usually give off a purple aura. Grey is, well, I've never heard of it before. The white hair sounds more like a side effect of witch magic. But the stone necklace you saw reflected sounds like a witch hunter artefact, though it would normally be made of metal.' She sat forward, her face troubled. 'Angelica must have used the powerful, combined witch and witch hunter spells in *Magic Most Dark* to get her revenge.'

Sophie shivered as she remembered the power of the spells in that book of dark magic, created by Angelica and Robert Lloyd to protect themselves from witches and witch hunters alike. She put her head in her hands. 'This is so awful,' she said, without looking up. 'I don't understand how she's become so warped and twisted. I thought she was acting out of love for Robert. But this isn't love, this is hatred!'

Katy gave her shoulder a quick shove, and Sophie

looked up in surprise. Callum was standing next to them, smiling at Katy.

'Oh – um – hi, Callum! I didn't hear you come in.'

'Stealthy as a ninja, that's me,' Callum said. He sat down next to them, running a hand through his hair so it stood up on end. 'So what were you two talking about? I heard something about spells and love and hatred. Sounds dramatic!'

'Um, er . . . ' Sophie looked around for inspiration and saw the bookshelf. 'It's a book! Katy and I were just talking about the, er, plot of a book we were reading.'

'Yeah!' Katy nodded enthusiastically. 'Um, it's about witches, and . . . stuff.'

'Yeah, stuff,' Sophie echoed. 'It's really good.'

'Oh, yeah?' Callum put his feet up on the opposite chair. 'Can I borrow it?'

Sophie stared at him, her mouth open with horror. She waved her hands vaguely. 'Um, n—'

'Yes!' said Katy brightly. Sophie choked with surprise. 'Yes, you totally can. I would love you to read it.' Katy beamed up at him. 'It's such a great book. It's sooo romantic. The heroine's a witch, and she's in love with this boy but he isn't a witch, he's a human, and so they think they can never be together, and it's just all about finding your true love, and it's so emotional, and there's a whole series. Maybe you've seen the first one? It's got a pink cover—'

Callum looked panicked. 'Um, actually, I'm more into elves than witches, really. And not so much into romance.'

Sophie caught Katy's eye and bit her cheeks to stop herself laughing. Katy giggled.

'You and your elves! Well, I guess I can let you off this time.' She pushed him playfully. 'Maybe you'd like me more if I had pointy ears?'

'I don't think so! Maybe you'd like me more if I acted like one of your soppy romance heroes?' Callum teased, pushing her back.

'Hmm, maybe!'

'Oh, thanks very much!' Callum tossed a cushion at her, grinning. Katy giggled and threw the cushion back. Callum batted it away.

Sophie managed a smile, but she felt a little

awkward as Katy and Callum went on flirting. To her relief the bell rang.

'Time for Biology!' Sophie jumped up, then wondered if she'd been a bit too enthusiastic as Katy and Callum looked at her in surprise.

She started off down the corridor and Katy ran to catch her up.

'You know, I feel so happy when I'm with Callum,' Katy said. 'I can't believe how lucky I am to be going out with him – it feels like all my problems just melt away when we're together.'

'Must be true love,' Sophie said, managing a smile.

'I think it is. And it's all thanks to you.' Katy slipped an arm into Sophie's and gave her a squeeze. 'I was so unhappy and lonely when I came to Turlingham, but everything's so much better now. I have the *best* best friend and the best boyfriend in the world – how lucky am I?' She laughed.

Sophie smiled for real this time. She decided she didn't mind feeling a bit left out if it meant Katy could be this truly happy!

'Well, I think you make Callum happy too – I've

never seen him spend so long away from a computer screen! It's like magic,' she added with a grin.

'Better than magic!' Katy laughed.

They filed into the Biology lab with their class-mates, dumped their bags on the bench and hopped up onto the lab stools.

Katy turned around to chat to Kaz and Joanna, but Sophie didn't join in. A huge, exciting thought had just hit her and knocked everything else out of her head.

Perched on the lab stool, she stared at the diagram of the heart Mrs Stevens had drawn on the board. *Better than magic.* What if love really was better than magic – or stronger, at least? What if *love* was the key to saving her grandmother?

The next morning Sophie came downstairs in her pyjamas and dressing gown to find her mum blow-drying her hair with one hand and fixing her earring with the other.

'Hello, darling,' she said, 'I'm late for the staff meet-ing – Franklin, can you make sure Sophie gets some breakfast?'

'I can get my own,' Sophie told her.

But her dad smiled at her and said, 'Come on, you haven't tasted a pancake till you've had one of my specials.'

'Hmm, well, if you put it like that!' Sophie sat down at the kitchen table with a grin. As she watched her father put a frying pan on the Aga to heat up, and crack eggs into a bowl, she couldn't help thinking that all these ten years they could have been making pancakes together, if only he'd been there ... But he was back again now and that was all that mattered. Besides, she had a plan she was sure could put everything right.

The door closed behind her mother, and she took a deep breath. This was the moment to tell her dad about it.

'Dad,' she said, 'I've been thinking more about it and I'm sure I'm right. We've just got to get Angelica and Robert back together.' She paused, but her father went on whisking the eggs as if he hadn't heard her. 'Don't you see? If Angelica and Robert are together again, they'll be happy. Angelica won't have any reason to be angry with Grandma, and she'll forgive her and take the curse off her. I mean, love is the strongest magic of all, isn't it?'

Still not speaking, her father crossed the kitchen, grabbed the cinnamon jar and strode back to the bowl.

'You aren't old enough to understand love yet.' He shook a big helping of the spice into the mixture.

'What?' Sophie cast a disbelieving glance at him. 'Could you get any more patronising?'

'I'm sorry, Sophie, but it's true. And besides,' he went on, 'how exactly do you propose to get her and Robert back together? You don't even know where they are.'

'But we can find out!' Sophie said. 'Katy could help us use some witch hunter method to help us find Angelica.'

Sophie's father sighed. Without looking at her, he muttered, 'It's best not to involve outsiders in witch business. I can handle my sister.' He poured the mixture into the pan and it began to spatter.

'But Katy's not an outsider!' Sophie said, her hands

on her hips. 'Angelica tried to hurt her, too. She's just as involved as we are.'

Her father stood silently as he flipped the pancakes over and over. His face was troubled.

'You don't understand,' he said finally. He slid the pancakes onto a plate and passed them to her.

'No, I don't!' Sophie stared at him. 'I don't get why—'

'I'll leave you to enjoy your pancakes,' said her father. He strode to the door, shoulders hunched, and left without a backward glance.

Sophie stared after him, open-mouthed with shock. She was annoyed to find her lip wobbling and her eyes filling with tears. Her father had only been home a few days and he was already messing up her dreams of a happy family.

Father and daughter witch team? Maybe not.

Sophie bent over her History rough book and scribbled a note to Katy, glancing up now and then to check that Mr McGowan wasn't looking. He wasn't, but Erin was. Sophie gave her a smile and went on writing:

I don't get why he doesn't get it! she finished. *It makes sense to use witch hunting methods to find Angelica.*

As soon as she was sure Erin wasn't looking, she folded the note up small and passed it to Katy.

Katy's face grew solemn as she read the note. Then she began to write on the other side. Sophie waited impatiently until the note came back to her. On the other side, Katy had written:

I get it. He doesn't want to work with a witch hunter – ANY witch hunter. Well, would you, if you were him?

Sophie looked up in shock and met Katy's eyes. Katy gave a tiny, sad shrug.

Sophie opened her mouth to protest but was stopped by Mr McGowan. 'Sophie, what's that on your desk?'

Sophie reddened and hid the note under her book. 'Nothing, sir.'

'Good. Because if it was a note I would be reading it out for the whole class to hear.' He raised an eyebrow as a warning.

Sophie breathed a long sigh of relief.

Maybe Katy had a point. Her father had been on the run from witch hunters for years. Ten years, separated from his wife and daughter, and most of it, she knew, caused by Katy's own family. There was no way it would be easy for him to accept Katy, but that didn't mean it was impossible.

She folded the note up again and slipped it into her pencil case. There was just one thing to do, then. Because she knew for certain that she wasn't giving up!

The bell went for lunch, and Sophie grabbed Katy's arm as they went out of the classroom.

'We've got to talk,' she began, but quickly fell silent as Erin and Kaz hurried up to them.

'Hey, what were you two passing notes about in the lesson then? Share the goss!' Erin said, nudging Sophie with her elbow.

'Yeah, you looked all serious!' Kaz chimed in.

'Oh, um . . . ' Sophie looked at Katy, feeling guilty. There was no way she could tell the truth, and it felt awful to lie to her friends.

'Hey, there go Mark and Oliver!' Katy said quickly, pointing down the corridor.

'Where?' Erin and Kaz spun round, and Sophie quickly pulled Katy into the girls' toilets. Looking under the cubicle doors she could see the toilets were empty.

'I know what to do,' Sophie said, tensing her shoulders in excitement.

'What? Hypnotise your dad? Hold him at gunpoint?' Katy smiled, but her eyes were sad. 'He doesn't want to work with a Gibson.'

'He doesn't trust you,' Sophie agreed. 'But that's because he doesn't know you. We just have to prove to him that our plan will work.'

'How?' Katy raised her eyebrows.

Sophie smiled. 'If you and me can fix things, that will prove to my dad that witches and witch hunters can work together!'

Katy stared at her with her mouth open. A slow smile broke across her face. 'Are you sure? Your dad won't approve . . . '

'He will when he sees our plan works!' Sophie headed for the door. 'Come on – let's get started!'

They raced out of the toilets.

'Hey, Sophie, Katy – where are you going?' Erin called after them.

'Um – tell you later!' Sophie tossed over her shoulder as they hurried towards the hall and up the stairs to the girls' dorms. She hoped Erin wouldn't remember to ask.

Katy led the way into her dormitory. Sophie shut the door and put her back against it. Gally scampered out of her bag and sniffed around the room.

'Now, let me think – I know there was a spell to find any named witch in *Magic Most Dark*.' Sophie frowned, thinking hard. 'But we don't have the book.'

'We won't need it.' Katy opened her wardrobe and took out a suitcase. She lugged it over to her bed and opened it. Inside were phials and vials, curious-looking twisted bits of metal pipe, and bottles containing smoke and shimmering powders. 'My parents are so annoyed with me for not finding the Turlingham Witch yet that they made me revise a whole load of witch-seeking methods at half term, after you left.' She began sorting through the equipment, picking out bits of pipe and vessels that looked to Sophie like parts from some very weird Meccano set. 'I'm sure I can remember how to do this ... pass me that atlas, would you?' She pointed to a dog-eared atlas lying on her chest of drawers.

Sophie picked up the atlas and brought it over. Meanwhile, Katy had set out a row of vials and bottles on her desk. She carefully began to mix them in a glass container which she had set on a stand. The room began to fill with an odd smell.

'Are you sure it's safe to do this now?' Sophie glanced at the door: Mrs Freeman might walk in at any moment. She couldn't imagine the trouble if she saw them playing with fire in the dorms.

'If we're quick!' Katy continued pouring the ingredients into the container, alternately stirring and chanting.

'*Umbra aut luce, die aut nocte.* Bring the witch we seek to sight!'

Gally sat close by, quivering slightly and sniffing the air uncomfortably. The liquid bubbled, and a purple aura steamed off it.

'It's nearly ready!' Katy turned to Sophie. 'Can you find a prism in my bag? And put the atlas down on the bed, open at the page that shows the whole world.'

Sophie looked in Katy's bag and found a small, slightly chipped prism. She held it out, and Katy carefully poured the muddy liquid over it and onto the page, chanting: 'Day and night, dark and light. Let Gertrude Poulter come to sight!'

The liquid separated into streams of shimmering colours as it ran over the prism and splashed onto the page. Whorls of colour ran around as if they were searching for something and, finally, came together in one glowing drop – just underneath the pink shape of England.

'What's that? What's it on?' Sophie and Katy bumped heads as they craned to see.

Katy tipped the paper slightly so she could see what was under the liquid. 'It's an island … between England and France.'

'The Channel Islands,' said Sophie. She turned the pages until they got to a more detailed map of the Channel Islands, and Katy tried the incantation again.

The murky liquid flowed around the page like mercury in water once more, then finally came to rest. Sophie peered at the writing. 'Jersey!' She looked up at Katy. 'We've found her! Angelica's in Jersey.'

'It worked,' Katy said, and seemed proud of herself.

'Come on, lunch is almost over.' Sophie grabbed Katy's arm. 'And we've got to show Dad how brilliant you are.'

As they ran towards the cottage, Sophie saw her father come out of the front door, wrapped up in his dark coat. He was heading towards the woods. She sped up and Katy followed her.

'Dad!' Sophie gasped, a stitch in her side. Her father had turned onto a path in the woods, his head down as if he were thinking hard. 'Wait!'

'Sophie?' He turned around, startled. His face seemed to close over as he saw Katy. 'Shouldn't you two be in school?'

Sophie could only pant and hold out the atlas, open to the page where the liquid still hovered.

'What's this?' He looked at the map.

'It's, um, a witch hunter thingy . . . ' Katy began.

'I can see that.' Sophie's father waved away the purple aura that was beginning to form above the page.

'She did it,' Sophie burst out. 'Katy found Angelica. She's in Jersey!'

Her father examined the map. His forehead furrowed, and a wary expression came into his eyes.

'Now we just have to find Robert,' Sophie went on. 'Then get them together. And we'll save Grandma!'

Sophie's dad frowned. 'I've already told you,' he said. 'I don't want you going anywhere near Robert Lloyd.' He handed the atlas back to Sophie and glanced from Sophie to Katy. 'Do you . . .?' He sighed. 'Have you considered that he might have helped Angelica put the curse on your grandmother?'

Sophie shook her head. 'His image didn't appear in the water, remember?'

Her father coughed hurriedly and glanced at Katy.

Sophie pushed on. 'He's got no reason to. Why would he harm Grandma?' But Sophie was beginning to question herself.

'*Reason?*' Her father frowned. 'He's a witch hunter. They hate us! They're pure . . . '

Sophie felt herself turning red. She didn't dare speak, but she hoped her expression said it all.

'I – er – apologise,' he growled, looking at Katy but not looking sorry at all. 'That wasn't fair. But, anyway,' he added, gesturing to the atlas, 'you must have made a mistake.'

'A *mistake*?' Sophie and Katy said together. They exchanged a look of disbelief.

'How do you—' Sophie started.

'No witch with half a brain would go near Jersey at this time of year. It would be suicide.' He cast a quick glance up and down the path. In a low voice, he went on: 'Every year there is an important gathering of the witch hunter families in the Channel Islands. The witch community believes it's happening in the next few weeks.'

Sophie turned to Katy. 'Katy? Is that true?'

'I do remember my parents talking about some big meeting coming up,' Katy said, slowly. She shook her head. 'Your dad's right. I must have made some kind of mistake with the potion. Maybe I got the mixture wrong.' Sophie could see tears in her eyes.

'I think so,' said Sophie's dad. He turned away. 'Now you two should be back in school, and I've got to . . . ' Pausing before he walked on, he added, 'I – er – appreciate your efforts, though.'

They watched him walk away into the woods, his boots crunching on the frosty ground.

Katy sighed, her bottom lip trembling. 'Sorry, Sophie. I wish I knew where I went wrong.'

'No way!' Sophie said. 'You didn't get it wrong. You're better than that, Katy.' She scowled after her father's distant figure. 'Even if my father doesn't realise it.'

Sophie was determined to prove to her dad that he was mistaken about her best friend.

'But he will,' she finished.

FIVE

Sophie bounced up and down on the tips of her toes to keep warm. Even the seagulls on the roof of Bowden Hospital looked as if they were shivering.

'Come on, Mrs Freeman,' Erin groaned, 'let's get this party started! I'm f-f-f-f-freeeezing!'

Sophie grinned, glad all her friends had decided to join in with the vegetable garden project. Erin and Mark were hand in hand, and Kaz and Oliver were plugged into the same iPod, nodding their heads. Callum sat perched on the water butt on the other side of the garden, unaware that Gally was sitting on a branch behind him. Katy, Lauren and Joanna were near Sophie, rubbing their gloved hands together in the cold.

'OK, gardeners, are we all here?' Mrs Freeman looked at the huddle of students. 'Good. Let's get started. Our aim today is to get the vegetable garden cleared, planted and ready for winter.'

Sophie looked at the patch of ground she was pointing at. It was overgrown with weeds. Beanpoles leaned at sad angles and rubbish had blown onto it.

'We have to clear all that?' Erin sounded horrified.

'You'll be working in pairs; each pair will have responsibility for a single square of the garden.' Mrs Freeman pointed to strings that marked the garden into a grid.

Sophie smiled at Katy. They'd definitely be a pair.

Mrs Freeman looked around. 'Now, get into your pairs.' A few people started shuffling around. 'Oh, I forgot to say,' Mrs Freeman added, 'the pairs must be boy-girl.'

Sophie's face fell. She turned round, looking for

Callum. Apart from Katy, he was her best friend. 'Hey, Callum, over here!' She waved, and then watched as Callum winced. Sophie could have hit herself for being so stupid: of course Callum and Katy would want to work together.

'Maybe we can work in a three?' she suggested as Callum reached them.

'That's a good idea.' Katy nodded.

Callum put his hand up. 'Mrs Freeman,' he called out. 'Please can we be a three?'

Maggie Millar, looking their way, scowled. 'Absolutely not!'

'We weren't asking you,' Callum said, and Maggie scowled harder. 'Mrs Freeman?'

'A three? No, you may not.' Mrs Freeman shook her head. 'The whole point is that you should be in equal groups. A three would have an unfair advantage.'

Sophie sighed. 'Never mind. I'll find someone else,' she told them, and Katy looked disappointed as she walked away.

'See you later, Soph.'

Sophie looked around the allotment. Mark and

Erin were in a pair, of course, and so were Kaz and Oliver. Lauren and Joanna had paired up with boys, as well. There were a lot of boys she didn't know at all, but they already seemed to have found themselves partners, too. With a sinking feeling, Sophie began to see that she was going to be the odd one out.

She hadn't realised how much things would change once Katy started going out with Callum.

At the far end of the allotment she saw a huddle of Year 10 girls all jostling each other. She wondered what they were doing and then saw a tall figure pushing his way out from the middle of the group. Ashton. The girls followed him as he strode across the allotment, all begging him to be their partner. Sophie froze. He was coming her way. She looked around for somewhere to hide and hurried towards a tumbledown shed.

'Sophie!' Ashton broke into a run. 'Sophie!'

He caught up and tapped her on the shoulder, and all Sophie could do was slump in defeat. She turned round and Ashton smiled at her.

'Can I pair with you?'

Sophie caught a glimpse of the Year 10 girls scowling at her from a distance. She could sort of understand their feelings: Ashton was looking cuter than usual today, in his woolly hat and flight jacket. She wished she could explain to them that there was no need to worry – the only reason he wanted to pair with her was so he could try and trick her into revealing she was a witch.

She had just opened her mouth to tell him to get lost, when Mrs Freeman trotted by.

'In a pair, you two? Good.' She thrust a set of gardening tools into Sophie's hands.

'No, we're—' Sophie tried to thrust them back at her.

'Yes,' Ashton interrupted with a grin. 'Thank you, Mrs Freeman.'

'But—' Sophie tried.

Mrs Freeman wasn't listening. She took out a whistle and blew it so loudly that Sophie winced.

'Right, you lot,' she shouted across the garden, 'time starts now! Off you go!'

Sophie groaned. 'Come on then, let's get this over with.'

'Way to make a guy feel appreciated,' Ashton murmured.

Sophie was too annoyed to reply.

Sophie pulled up a handful of weeds, imagining it was Ashton's hair.

'That's a nice ring you're wearing,' he said. 'You never take it off, do you?'

Sophie bit back a snarky reply. She'd been looking forward to today so much, and now it was spoiled: instead of working with her best friend, she was stuck with the most annoying boy in the world. With him watching her, she couldn't risk using even a tiny bit of magic, or letting Gally help plant a seed or two.

Suddenly she couldn't be bothered to play his games any more. He must have known the ring was her Source – he'd be stupid not to.

'Yeah, I never take it off,' she said. 'I *sourced* it from a local market. Apparently it came from the *source* of the Nile . . . and I think it's pretty *saucy*, don't you?' She held up the ring so the stone caught the light and flashed at him.

Ashton gaped at her. He looked as if he'd had the ground whisked out from under him. Then he burst out laughing. 'I have to hand it to you,' he said, through his laughter. 'For a witch, you're pretty funny.'

'*If* I was a witch,' Sophie smirked, 'I'd take that as a compliment.'

Ashton chuckled, and Sophie bit back a smile as she tossed the weeds into the wheelbarrow. At least Ashton could laugh at himself.

As soon as the barrow was full, she grabbed the handles and wheeled it over to the compost heap. As she tipped the weeds onto the pile, Kaz came running over, followed by Joanna, Erin and Lauren.

'Sophie!' Kaz grabbed her arm, practically dancing with excitement, and pulled her aside. 'Ashton Gibson fancies you!' she said in a thrilled whisper.

'He chose you as his partner. That's so romantic!' Lauren chipped in, and Joanna nodded violently.

Erin finished. 'Oh my God, like, all the Year 10 girls want your *head*!'

Sophie let out a snort of disbelief. 'You're so wrong,' she said, firmly. 'Trust me.'

'Not only did he ask you to be his partner, but he was staring at you the whole time Mrs Freeman was talking!' Jo protested. 'If a boy stares at you, it means he likes you. I read it in a magazine.'

'Yeah, it definitely means he's into you!' Kaz agreed. 'What are you going to do, Sophie?'

Sophie laughed, feeling embarrassed and annoyed. 'I'm not going to do anything. Because he doesn't fancy me.'

'Oh, come on!' Erin burst out. 'Why would he stare at you like that, otherwise?'

'If you want the truth,' Sophie found herself saying, 'he's staring at me because he *hates* me. He's making my life a living hell!'

'Whaaaat?' Erin exclaimed. Her friends stared, mouths open. 'How could anyone hate you?'

Kaz frowned. 'You're unhateable, Sophie!'

Sophie smiled, feeling flustered. She'd said too much. But it felt good to get things off her chest. 'Who knows?' She shrugged. 'But he's constantly on my back, it's so annoying.'

'No way!' Kaz exclaimed. 'How dare he?'

Erin's eyes were wide. 'So *that's* why you and Katy keep passing notes and what you're whispering about. Oh, poor Sophie!' She hugged her. 'You could have told us, though – I feel so guilty now.'

'Guilty? Why?'

Erin exchanged an embarrassed look with the others.

'Well,' said Lauren, 'you and Katy seemed to be avoiding us, and we thought you had some big secret you didn't want to share – we didn't realise you were trying to figure out what to do about Ashton.'

Sophie gaped at her. She realised with a guilty shock that she and Katy probably had been making Erin and the others feel left out. But what could she do? She couldn't tell them the truth.

'What are you whispering about here?' Maggie Millar suddenly loomed over them, scowling. 'You should be working.'

Sophie jumped and looked up.

'Maggie,' Erin said, 'Sophie's being bullied.'

Sophie shook her head hurriedly. 'Erin, it's OK!'

'No, Sophie, you must tell someone,' Kaz went on.

'Maggie, it's Ashton Gibson in Year 10, he's pestering her and annoying her—'

'Is this true?' Maggie's expression hardened, and she whipped out her red notebook.

'Well, not exactly . . .' Sophie's face went burning hot.

'We don't stand for bullying at Turlingham. Would you like me to do something, Sophie?'

Sophie looked up in amazement. She'd never heard Maggie sound so nice. Maggie's pen hovered over her notebook.

Sophie swallowed. 'Um, no. Thank you, Maggie, but it's fine.' Erin opened her mouth to protest but Sophie shook her head at her. 'It isn't a big deal. Honestly.'

'It's much better to—' Maggie started, but Sophie had grabbed the empty wheelbarrow and steered it away from them.

'I'm really, really sure. Thanks anyway, Maggie.'

She headed back to Ashton, wishing her face was less red. Maggie meant well, but the last thing Sophie needed was extra attention from the head prefect.

*

'I know I'm going to regret asking this,' said Erin, her voice muffled through the hand she'd put over her mouth and nose, 'but what exactly *is* manure?'

Sophie stopped digging and leaned on her spade. She looked at Katy and they both giggled. At least they'd all managed to get patches next to each other. 'Um, Erin, there's no nice way to explain this,' she began. But before she could finish, Maggie, who was striding around the outside of the garden like a prison guard, shouted out: 'No slacking, Sophie! This has to be perfect for planting by the end of the day!'

Sophie sighed and went on digging. The ground was hard and frosty, but at least there weren't many stones in it. All around her, the other Turlingham students were working busily. Sophie glanced up to the hospital building on the crest of the hill. She wondered how her grandma was doing.

Erin walked by, complaining to Mark: 'I've got blisters already. And it's freezing! You'd have to be nuts to enjoy this.'

Sophie grinned to herself. She *did* enjoy it – she loved gardening. She'd loved it even before she'd discovered that she could work real magic on nature. She didn't even mind the manure.

Just as she was wondering if doing a little bit of magic would really be cheating – after all, it was for the patients – she saw a tall, balding man behind the trees. Although he wore a care-assistant's uniform, he was creeping around as if he didn't want to be seen. Then Sophie remembered where she had seen him before: he had been in her grandmother's room when they had come in to see her.

Sophie put down her spade and dusted off her hands. Perhaps the man would be able to tell her how her grandmother was doing. He looked kind.

In front of her, Ashton straightened up from his spade, breathing hard, and pushed his hair out of his eyes.

Sophie stopped dead, looking from Ashton to the male nurse. There was something about them that was similar ... She clapped a hand to her mouth to stifle a gasp. *Of course!* she thought. Now that she saw them next to each other, the family resemblance was unmistakeable. The man was Robert Lloyd! Even though she'd only seen him in a photo from twenty years ago, it was clearly the same man – Angelica's husband, and Katy and Ashton's second cousin. She had to tell Katy, fast.

'Hey, Sophie, wake up,' Ashton said. 'We've still got loads of work to do, you slacker!'

Sophie ignored him and turned to Katy, who was working beside her but on her own patch.

'Katy, I – I've got to go to the bathroom,' she said. 'Come with me? Please?' She took Katy's arm and started pulling her towards the hospital.

Ashton moved to block them. 'You've got to go right now? But there's loads left to do.'

'We won't be long,' Sophie said, steering Katy past him.

Ashton followed. 'I probably ought to come with you. To see you're safe,' he added, as Sophie looked at him in disbelief. 'After all, it's a mental hospital. I don't think—'

'Ahem – Ashton . . . '

Sophie jumped at the noise behind her. She had been too distracted to hear Maggie approaching.

'Sophie is perfectly capable of going to the bathroom on her own,' Maggie told Ashton with a stern frown. 'I've got my eye on you, young man,' she said, and pointed at him. 'Back to the garden. Sophie and Katy, be quick – there's a lot of work still to do on your patches.'

Ashton backed away, scowling. Sophie smiled a relieved smile at Katy, and they ran off up the path towards the hospital building. Maggie definitely had her uses!

'He went this way.' Sophie ran on tiptoe up the winding path, through the gardens towards the hospital. Katy followed her.

'But are you sure it was him?'

'Positive! I recognise him from the photo in your family album, and if you'd seen him standing next to Ashton – oh!' She stopped dead as she saw Robert Lloyd up ahead of them, and gestured to Katy to hide behind a bush.

Robert glanced around, then opened the back door of the hospital and hurried in.

'You're right, it *is* him – and I bet he's not supposed to be here. Look how he's hiding and sneaking around!' Katy whispered. 'What are we going to do?'

Sophie swallowed, but there was no point in chickening out now. 'We're going to speak to him!'

'What? Are you sure?'

'Why not? We can tell him we know where Angelica is. We have to get those two back together – otherwise there's no chance Angelica will soften and lift the curse. Come on!'

She ran to the door and followed Robert Lloyd inside and down the corridor. The corridor was deserted, though she could hear nurses' voices from deeper inside the building. She was about to call out to Robert when she felt Katy's hand on her arm.

'Let me speak first,' Katy whispered. 'I know he's an outcast but he's still a witch hunter – and we don't know how he feels about witches.'

Sophie realised Katy was right. Maybe Robert Lloyd would respond like her father had to Katy – or worse. She hung back in the shelter of a stairwell, and peered out to see Katy walk ahead.

'Um, excuse me?' Katy began.

Robert Lloyd jumped and spun around, his eyes wide and nervous.

'Hi!' Katy held out her hands. 'I wondered if—'

Robert frowned. He looked distracted. 'You're one of the Turlingham girls, aren't you?'

'Yes, I am. And . . . I know who you are.'

Sophie held her breath.

'W-what do you mean?'

'You're Robert Lloyd.' The man drew in his breath, and Katy hurried on. 'And you're my second cousin.'

Robert stared at her. 'How do you . . .' he began, then he paused. 'My goodness, yes. Look at you . . . Gibson through and through.'

Katy smiled and nodded. 'Katy. My mum is Fara Gibson.'

Robert Lloyd smiled, but it quickly fell from his face. He took a step back. 'Oh, no – you've been sent by your parents, haven't you?' He looked from left to right and Sophie had to duck further into the shadows so he wouldn't see her. 'What more do you want from us? You've driven us apart, isn't that enough for you? I know I followed Angelica here but you don't understand, I couldn't stay away, I love her—'

'Wait!' Katy broke in hurriedly. 'You've got the wrong idea. I'm not against witches and witch hunters being married, or friends, or – or whatever. In fact, I don't think they should be working against each other at all.'

Robert frowned. 'Really? And why should I believe you?'

'Because,' Katy cast a desperate glance towards Sophie, who stepped out of the shadows, and took a long, shaky breath. 'Because this is my best friend.'

Robert Lloyd looked round, and Sophie saw his eyes widen as he recognised her.

'My name's Sophie Morrow,' Sophie told him. 'And my father is Franklin Poulter.'

'Yes,' Robert Lloyd said slowly. 'I saw you with him the other day.'

He took a moment to stare at her, and Sophie could see by his expression it was all sinking in.

'I'm a witch, like my father ... and like my aunt,

Angelica.' She saw Robert flinch, and she went on, 'So that makes you my uncle.' She smiled an uncertain smile. 'And I want the same thing as you: I want to get our family back together.'

SIX

Robert Lloyd drew in his breath. To Sophie's astonishment, his eyes were full of tears.

'Are you OK?' Katy reached out for his arm, but he shook his head quickly and turned away. He drew out a handkerchief from his pocket and blew his nose. When he turned back, his eyes were still wet.

'I'm sorry,' he said, stuffing the handkerchief back in his pocket. 'I suppose it must seem pathetic, but even though the witches and witch hunters drove us apart, I can't forget her. She's the only woman I'll ever love. I've been trying to find her for so long. I thought she might come back to her family, but as far as I can tell she's nowhere near here.' He looked around him and lowered his voice. 'I faked some papers and got a job at the hospital. I'm just hoping she will come back to see her mother.'

Sophie and Katy exchanged a glance.

'I doubt that,' Sophie said. 'She's the one who put the curse on Grandma.'

'She is?' Robert's mouth fell open. 'Of course, she's under a spell from our book. Why didn't I see that?'

Sophie was a little surprised that he didn't seem more horrified at what Angelica had done, but there was no time to waste.

'You love Angelica, don't you?' she went on, eagerly.

'I love her more than anything in the world,' Robert said, sadly.

'Then you have to tell her how you feel!'

'But—'

'There are no buts!' Sophie said firmly. 'Love is the most important thing in the world, and I know she loves you, too!'

Robert twisted his fingers together nervously.

'But the witch hunters and the witches – they'll begin to persecute us again. They'll separate us again.'

'They may try, but if you truly love each other you can get through anything,' Sophie said, thinking of her parents.

Tears filled Robert's eyes. 'They tore us apart, and now I don't know where she is.'

Sophie and Katy exchanged a delighted grin.

'That,' said Sophie, 'is *not* a problem!'

Katy quickly explained how she had found Angelica. Robert listened, a look of keen interest on his face.

'I don't think I've ever heard of this method,' he said. 'So you mix the milk of magnesia with the calcium carbonate first, *before* adding the ground emeralds? But doesn't that decrease their effect?'

This was all *way* over Sophie's head.

'You'd think so,' said Katy, 'but actually it doesn't, because—'

'Um, guys.' Sophie was amused at the two witch

hunters talking shop, but they needed to get on. 'The point is, Robert, that Angelica's in Jersey. So what are you going to do about it?'

There was silence as both girls looked hopefully at Robert. He seemed to swell before their eyes, pulling himself upright.

'I'm going after her,' he whispered. He seemed to be looking through them, a distant light in his eyes. 'What we have together is too strong, too powerful, too important' – Sophie nodded enthusiastically: her plan was working brilliantly – 'if only you're sure she feels the same about me.'

Sophie was blank for an instant, then she smiled.

'I've got an idea!' She glanced towards the hospital's day room, which was empty. On the windowsill was a glass bowl full of roses. And next to the day room was the disabled toilet, which was also empty.

'Follow me.' Sophie ran into the day room. 'I'm going to try and cast a spell so that you can speak to her right now.' She wasn't going to let Robert change his mind.

She carried the bowl into the toilet, beckoning Katy

and Robert after her. She put the roses carefully on one side, poured away the old water and put fresh, clear water in. She handed the bowl to Robert.

'Look into the bowl,' she commanded.

'Okaaaay.' Robert peered into the bowl.

Sophie took a handful of the rose petals and rubbed them between her fingers so that their scent spread.

'I don't quite understand,' Robert began, looking up from the vase.

'The smell of roses is to get you into a romantic mood,' Sophie told him. 'You know, like in the Disney films. Only I promise not to sing!'

'Romantic?' Robert asked. 'Er – why?'

'So you'll be able to connect with Angelica better!'

'But Angelica's not here.'

'Ah, wait and see,' Sophie said with a grin. The rich scent of roses came up from her hands, and Sophie's finger tingled under her Source as the magic started to work. She was almost sure her idea would work; it was only slightly different from the spell her father had done, after all.

'Forces of the Earth, of the heavens above, let the water show clearly as a mirror, the one who he loves!'

A heady smell, like ripe strawberries and sweet jasmine and fresh night air, rolled out from the water. Robert sighed in pleasure as he breathed in the wave of scent, and closed his eyes. New roses bloomed on the stems Sophie had laid aside.

'Think of Angelica,' Sophie whispered to him. 'Think how much you love her.'

Robert breathed deeply, a gentle smile on his face. Then he gasped in astonishment. 'She's there – in the water!'

Katy peered over his shoulder. 'He's right! You did it, Sophie!'

Sophie quickly came to look into the bowl. In the water, Angelica's face had appeared, shimmering like oil on water. She was looking down, her head resting on one hand. She seemed to be writing at a desk. Beside her was a glass of water.

Sophie looked at Robert, who was staring open-mouthed into the bowl. Afraid that Angelica would hear her if she spoke, she nudged Robert.

'Angelica!' Robert yelled. Sophie put a finger to her lips, urging him to whisper. 'Angelica, darling – where are you? Are you safe?'

In the image in the water, Angelica jumped and dropped her pen.

'Robert?' she said, looking around her. 'Is that you? Where are you?' Her voice sounded muffled, as if they were hearing it from under water.

'Tell her to look into her water,' Sophie whispered.

'Look into the glass, Angelica,' Robert told her.

Angelica turned and stared into the water. 'Robert!' A look of delight came over her face. 'It's so good to see you again! My darling, how are you?'

'I'm OK. I've been worrying about you and missing you so much. Angelica, we mustn't let them keep us apart any longer.'

Sophie and Katy tapped hands in a silent high five.

'Oh, Robert!' Angelica clasped her hands together. 'How did you find me? How did you break the curse that has kept us apart?'

'Never mind that now, it's complicated.' Robert

pressed on. 'Where are you? I'm going to come and find you.'

'Jersey.' Angelica laughed.

'Jersey?' Robert's face clouded. 'But it's terribly dangerous! You must leave now. The Gathering of the Thirteen Families is next weekend.'

'I know,' Angelica said with a strange smile. 'That's why I'm here.'

Robert shot a quick glance at Katy and Sophie, but Sophie shook her head. Angelica mustn't know they were there. 'Angelica . . . what are you planning?'

'Isn't it obvious?' Her smile was wide and manic. 'I have *Magic Most Dark* – the spells we created of a magic so powerful that most witches and witch hunters wouldn't even believe could exist. I intend to use it to destroy the witch hunter families – every last one of them!'

Sophie bit back a gasp. Destroying the witch hunter families meant destroying Katy's family . . . destroying Katy. There was no way she could let that happen.

SEVEN

Katy clapped her hand to her mouth, the fear evident in her eyes. Robert Lloyd's face was frozen – Sophie couldn't read his expression.

'What was that noise?' Angelica cocked her head. 'You are alone, aren't you, Robert?'

'Of course I am,' Robert said quickly. 'Angelica, this is an ... extraordinary plan.'

'Isn't it?' Angelica grinned gleefully, and her eyes sparked with a crazed light. 'With all the chief witch hunter families together, we can get rid of them all in one go!'

'But how? How are you planning to do this?'

'A Spell of Obliteration.' A large grin appeared on her face.

Katy turned pale.

Sophie quickly held her hand. She wasn't entirely sure what obliteration was, but it did *not* sound good.

'It's so perfect,' Angelica's voice was slow and dreamy. 'You will help me, won't you, Robert?'

Katy and Sophie exchanged a horrified glance. Angelica was mad after all. Robert had to do the right thing and stop her.

Instead of answering Angelica's question, Robert said, 'I'm going to come to you. Please, don't do anything before I get there.'

'Don't worry. I wouldn't want you to miss a moment of this. Dear Robert,' said Angelica, her voice softening further. 'It's good to hear your voice. I've missed you ever since my despicable mother drove us apart.'

'I've missed you, too,' Robert said sadly. He kissed the tips of his fingers and reached out to her image but, as the water rippled, her image disappeared.

'She's insane.' Sophie broke the silence. 'I'm sorry, Robert, but she must be.'

Robert nodded, his face looking old and worried. 'I agree. I've never heard her sound like that before. Angelica's not a murderer . . . ' He paused. 'My family will be there, too – they may have disowned me, but this just can't happen!'

Sophie sighed in relief.

'She'll never succeed – she'll be caught, and demag-icked, or killed,' Robert went on, now pacing up and down. 'No, we have to stop her.'

'What about my parents?' Katy blurted, her lip trem-bling. 'They're going to be there.' She looked at Sophie. 'I might not agree with what they do, but they're my *parents*! I don't want them to be ob-ob-obliterated!'

'Don't worry, Katy,' Sophie said, putting her arm around her. 'We will stop her. We've got to, haven't we, Robert?'

'Of course,' said Robert. 'I must get to Jersey – I must go at once.' He turned and strode out.

Sophie watched him go with a mixture of relief and fear. If only he could bring Angelica to her senses!

She started as the pendulum clock on the wall struck three.

'Three?' she exclaimed. 'Oh, no – the gardening session ends at three!' She turned to Katy. 'We'd better run, before Maggie catches us.'

Sophie raced through the gardens. As she came through a gap between some rhododendrons, she saw Callum and Ashton in the distance. Callum's arms were folded, and Ashton was pacing up and down. She could tell they were annoyed.

'Uh-oh,' Katy muttered as they drew closer. 'I think we're in trouble!'

Ashton strode towards them, scowling. Callum stood silently, but Sophie could tell he was upset.

'Where have you been?' Ashton demanded. 'You said you were going to the bathroom – you've been gone an hour! I had to do all the work!' He gestured at the patch. Like Callum and Katy's, it had been worked on, but it wasn't anywhere near finished. 'There's no way we'll pass the award now.' Ashton kicked at the ground.

'I – I wasn't feeling well,' Sophie said. Her stomach *was* churning, out of guilt. 'I'm sorry, Ashton. I didn't mean to skive.'

'Yeah, right,' Ashton sneered. He turned on Katy. 'You ought to be ashamed, hanging around with her when you know perfectly well what she is!' Katy stared at the ground, turning pink. 'You're a disgrace to the Gibsons!'

'Hey!' Sophie looked up to see Callum striding towards them. She had never seen him look so angry: his ears were pink and his fists were clenched. 'Shut it,' he snapped at Ashton as he reached them. 'Leave them alone.'

Ashton looked him up and down. 'What's it got to do with you?'

'Everything. Sophie's my best friend and Katy's my girlfriend. And if you insult them again I'll make you pay,' Callum replied.

Ashton gulped. 'Your *girl*friend? You're telling me you're going out with my sister?' He turned to Katy. 'What do you think you're at Turlingham for? Fun? You'd better focus, and fast.' He glanced at Callum, then looked back at Katy and snorted. 'I knew you had bad taste in friends; seems your taste in boyfriends is about the same.'

'Oi!' Callum jumped forwards, trembling with anger, and grabbed Ashton's arm, but Ashton shook him off and strode away, pulling off his gardening gloves and flinging them down as he went. As he trampled across the newly dug furrows, he turned and pointed at Sophie, shouting: 'And *you* can explain to Mrs Freeman exactly why our patch is so rubbish!'

Sophie watched miserably as Ashton stormed off towards the minibus. She turned back as she heard Katy say, 'Thanks, Callum.'

'Yeah, thanks for sticking up for us,' Sophie said. 'And I'm really sorry we were gone so long.'

Callum nodded stiffly, his hands plunged in his pockets and his thin shoulders hunched. 'Were you really feeling ill?' he asked.

Sophie hesitated. Lying to Ashton was one thing, but Callum was like her brother. Lying to him felt terrible.

Callum nodded slowly, his mouth turning down in

a sad line. 'I didn't think so,' he said. He turned to Katy. 'Why was your brother so rude? He had a real attitude about Sophie. What's going on?'

Katy glanced at Sophie, who cringed, unable to think of a good explanation.

'Um ...' Katy began, and then tailed off. Callum looked back and forth between the girls.

'I wouldn't have minded you going off if you'd told me what you were really doing,' he said, pushing his glasses up his nose and hunching his shoulders even more. 'I mean, Ashton's right – we're never going to pass the Silver Award now.'

Sophie looked at the patches. She had to agree they looked pretty bad. Ashton had destroyed their new furrows as he'd stormed off, half of it wasn't even weeded, and the seeds weren't planted.

She reached for her gardening gloves but, as she did so, a whistle cut through the air.

'Down tools, girls and boys,' Mrs Freeman called across the allotment. 'The session's over – I'll be coming round to check your patches and see how you did.'

Sophie heard Callum say, 'Katy, won't you at least tell me where you were all day?'

Katy's face was miserable, but she just shrugged and turned away.

Sophie's heart ached. Callum looked just as hurt and confused as her mother had done when she'd walked out of the sitting room, away from their father.

If Katy couldn't tell Callum the truth, Sophie realised, it might ruin their relationship, too.

EIGHT

As soon as Sophie shut her bedroom door behind them, Katy slumped onto her bed, hugging her pillow.

'Ugh. That might rank as the worst day of my life ever,' she groaned.

'It wasn't great,' Sophie had to admit. 'We've failed the Silver Award – which means no Holland trip.'

'I don't care about the Holland trip. It was just awful having to lie to Callum!' Katy buried her face in the pillow and went on, muffled: 'I feel so horrible.

Oh, Sophie, his face! I'm the worst girlfriend in the world. He's going to dump me, for sure.'

'He won't!' Sophie sat next to her and put a comforting hand on her shoulder. 'You couldn't possibly have told him the truth, Katy – you know that. It's not your fault.' She paused, remembering her parents again. It would be beyond awful if Katy and Callum were torn apart the way her mum and dad had been. And it would be just as bad for her to lose Callum's friendship.

'Let's not think about it,' Katy said, sitting up straight. 'It's too late to fix it, anyway. What about Angelica? What are we going to do to stop her? I can't let her destroy my parents!'

Sophie hugged her knees and thought hard. 'We've got to go to Jersey. But how are we going to manage that? Perhaps Dad could—'

'Girls!' Sophie's mum shouted from the bottom of the stairs. 'Dinner's ready!'

Katy and Sophie found the kitchen filled with the smell of cooking. A pan of spaghetti bubbled on the hob and the windows had steamed up. Sophie's mum, an apron tied loosely around her, was stirring the pasta sauce.

'I'll head off back to school,' Katy said. 'Free time is over and Mrs Freeman gets cross if we're late for dinner.'

Sophie was just walking Katy to the door when she noticed there were only two sets of cutlery on the table. 'Mum, where's Dad?'

'Your guess' – her mother placed the water glasses down firmly on the table – 'is as good as mine on that one.'

'What?' said Sophie.

Sophie's mum's voice was brittle. 'He's gone. Disappeared. Just as . . . as I was starting to get used to him—' Sophie's mum broke off and snatched up a piece of kitchen roll to blow her nose. 'I'm sorry, I have to . . . ' She hurried out of the room, but not before Sophie saw the tears rolling down her face.

Sophie started crying, too. Her dad had totally blown it with her mum. There was no way she would ever take him back again.

*

The first lesson on Monday was Geography. Sophie stared at the map of the British Isles on the wall. She focused on the tiny, important dot on the map, well below Britain. How were they going to get there and stop Angelica's horrible plan? She suddenly realised Mr Powell was asking her a question, and blurted out without thinking, 'Jersey.'

Mr Powell stared at her in disbelief, and her friends fell about in laughter.

'Er – not *precisely*, Sophie. Are you awake this morning?' Mr Powell raised an eyebrow. 'Can anyone else tell me which European country is also known as the Low Lands? I'll give you a clue: some of you will be going there on the Earl of Turlingham Gold Award expedition.'

Hands shot into the air, and Sophie's eyes widened. That was it! That was how to get to Jersey – the award expedition!

She waited until the bell had rung and then, as everyone was getting up to go to the next lesson, she made her way over to Katy.

'Listen, Katy,' she whispered, as they went out into

the corridor. 'I've been thinking. I know I don't know Dad very well but I'm sure he wouldn't walk out on us again. Maybe he's gone after Angelica. Maybe he finally believes that she's in Jersey and he's about to walk into danger.'

'Maybe,' said Katy, glancing around to check no one was listening.

'We've got to get to Jersey, and I know how,' Sophie said. 'We've got to get on the Gold Award trip.'

'It's the same weekend as the Gathering,' Katy said, nodding slowly. 'But, um, Sophie? The award's going to *Holland*. Holland? Jersey? Don't know if you know this, but they're not the same place.'

Sophie gave a triumphant grin. 'So, we just arrange that it doesn't go to Holland – it goes to Jersey instead!'

'That's a brilliant idea,' said Katy, now dodging around the flow of students heading to their classes, 'except for two things. One, we didn't pass the Silver Award, so we won't be going on the Gold Award trip, whether it's in Holland or Jersey or outer space. And two, how on earth are we going to get the trip moved to Jersey?'

Callum and Oliver were heading towards them, Callum beaming at Katy, so Sophie only had time to whisper: 'I'm a witch. You're a witch hunter. It's time to do what we do best!'

Katy laughed, her eyes on Callum. 'You mean . . . '

'. . . time to do some magic!' said Sophie. 'Meet you after school, and bring your wellies,' she finished under her breath, then smiled as Callum and Oliver said hello.

NINE

Sophie picked her way across the slippery rocks. The girls hadn't been able to meet until after the boarders' dinner and it was getting dark, but Katy's red coat stood out against the blue-grey sea and the cloudy sky. Seagulls squealed and circled: one perched close by, eyeing her hopefully.

Sophie took a few more steps and then stopped as she caught a glimpse of some green algae on a rock, among the cockles and winkles.

'Katy!' she called, waving. 'I've found some!'

Katy paused and turned round. As she made her way back towards Sophie, Sophie crouched down and scraped the algae off the rock with her finger, into the Petri dish that she'd borrowed from the Biology lab that afternoon. 'Yuck,' she muttered, as the green stuff slid into the dish.

'There's a cave over there we can use to do the spell,' Katy said as she reached her. She pointed to a black crack in the cliff.

Sophie followed her, making sure not to spill the algae.

They scrambled into the cave, where it was damp and cool, and so dark they could only just see. Sophie sat down on a rock, and Katy crouched near to her. Sophie carefully put the algae down between them.

'OK, now if my glamorous assistant would like to pass me the final ingredient?' She held out her hand to Katy. Katy giggled as she passed her a bottle of dark blue food colouring. Sophie dripped a few drops onto the algae, and it quickly turned a bluish-green colour.

'I've never helped with a witch spell before,' Katy said as she watched the algae. 'It's exciting!'

'I wonder if this is how Angelica and Robert started,' Sophie said thoughtfully. 'Helping each other with spells and then combining their magic into a new, more powerful sort. Wouldn't it be cool if we could do the same? I mean, combine our magic? But into a book called *Magic Most Light*, not *Magic Most Dark*.'

'Cool, but a bit scary!' Katy shivered. 'Anyway, we don't know how to.'

'No, and ordinary magic is difficult enough as it is!'

Sophie picked up the Petri dish and circled it so the algae and the food colouring mixed. 'Forces of the Earth,' she chanted, 'earth, water, wind and fire. Make this algae grow and fly until it reaches . . . ' She glanced at Katy, who was holding the brochure for the camping ground in Holland where the Gold Award team were to stay.

'Camping Egmondzee,' Katy read out, frowning over the difficult name.

'Camping Egmondzee.' Sophie circled the dish faster and faster, repeating the chant. Her Source glowed with a silvery light in the dark cave and she felt tingling waves of magic ripple through her. The algae floated up out of the dish, and fluttered like a bluey-green butterfly to the mouth of the cave. The girls ran after it, and watched as it vanished into the grey sky.

'I hope that's the right direction for Holland!' Katy said.

'And I hope the spell lasts long enough to work!' Sophie stared into the distance, but the algae was gone. She was worried. If this didn't work, she was out of ideas. 'After all, I didn't get my Source on my thirteenth birthday. I might just not be powerful enough yet.'

Katy reached out and squeezed her hand. 'No way. I believe in you – just like you believed in me.' She grinned.

They had the kind of faith in each other that only comes from being best friends.

'Tell you what, though,' Katy continued, 'can we go home and do something normal and totally not magical until I have to get back for curfew? Just for a change?'

'Definitely!' Sophie put up her hood as they left the cave; it had begun to drizzle. 'We could make cookies. I've got a great—'

'Um, yes, we could do that,' said Katy as she followed her up the cliff path. 'Or we could go and watch a film? Say, at Callum's house?'

Sophie laughed. 'How did I know you were going to say that? But first, let's stop by the library. There's a book I want to borrow ... for my mum.' The plan wouldn't be complete without it.

Sophie reached over to switch on the lamp as the image of a solemn elvish face faded away, and the credit music swelled. Katy, who'd been sitting forwards with her hands clasped and her eyes fixed on the screen, let out her breath in a big sigh.

'Wasn't it brilliant?' Callum turned to her, grinning. They were sitting on Callum's sofa and Sophie was pleased to see his arm was around Katy's back. 'Every time I see that film, it just gets better and better! How cool were those battle scenes?'

'Yeah, and the love story! It's just heartbreaking –

how they can never be together but he sacrifices everything, anyway.'

Sophie uncurled herself from her armchair. 'You two are elf crazy,' she said, hoping it didn't mean she'd be left out of more conversations. 'What shall we do now? Want to—'

'So what happens next?' Katy asked Callum, ignoring Sophie. 'Is there a sequel?'

'Guys, please can we—' Sophie started.

'There's a sequel,' Callum spoke over Sophie. 'But they haven't made the film yet. It should be out in a couple of years.'

'Guys?' Sophie tried again.

'A couple of years!' said Katy. 'But . . . '

As they carried on talking elf-nonsense, Sophie realised she might as well not have been there. Just then, her phone and Katy's both bleeped with messages.

Sophie pulled her phone out and read the message from Erin:

MARK DUMPED ME!!!! ☹ ☹

Her jaw dropped and when she looked over she saw Katy mirroring her expression as she read her own text. Katy looked up and met her eyes.

'It's from Erin—' Katy told Callum.

'—she's split up with Mark!' Sophie finished. She jumped to her feet. 'Sorry, Callum – we've got to get over to the dorm right now! This is an emergency!'

Katy texted as Sophie pulled on her coat. 'I'll just tell her we're coming.' Sophie put on her coat and hat and Katy went into the hall to put on her boots. As Sophie followed her, Callum caught her arm and pulled her back. 'Sophie! Can I talk to you quickly?' he whispered.

Sophie followed him back into the sitting room.

Callum pushed the door to and folded his arms. 'Look, Soph,' he began. 'I know Katy's hiding something from me. What is it? What's the big secret?'

'Um – nothing. Nothing. I don't know why you think that,' Sophie said, cringing inside with guilt.

'Oh, come on, Sophie!' Callum's voice was hurt. 'You're supposed to be my friend. I know something's going on; I'm not stupid.'

Sophie stared at her feet. She couldn't bear to lie to

Callum, but she couldn't tell him the truth, either. From the hall, she heard Katy calling her name.

'I've got to go. Sorry, Callum,' she mumbled. She pushed past him to get to the door.

'Fine,' Callum said, stepping aside. Sophie winced at the hurt in his voice. She followed Katy down the steps and into the cold. She turned back to wave, but Callum had already shut the door behind them.

As Sophie pushed open the doors at the end of the Year 9 corridor, she could already hear Erin wailing.

'Oh, no, poor Erin.' She ran down the corridor, Katy at her heels, and skidded to a halt at the common-room door. Through the glass panel she could see Joanna, Lauren and Kaz clustering around Erin. Crumpled tissues were scattered like confetti.

Sophie and Katy pushed open the door and went in.

'What happened?' Sophie said, running to Erin's side.

'How could he dump you?' Katy asked.

'Did he sell his brain on eBay or something?' Sophie added.

'Oh . . . ' Erin wiped her eyes with the tissue. 'We had an argument when we were working on the allotment. I mean,' she began, looking up at her friends, 'I just wanted to, like, chat about our relationship and stuff, but he just wanted to dig and get me to take photos of him posing with the spade.' She sniffed. 'And then we were hanging out together just now, and I just said how we were totally *Men Are From Mars, Women Are From Venus* – like, he doesn't even want to watch *America's Best Dance Crew*, he's just into soccer and there are not even any cheerleaders in that – and he said that since we were obviously from different planets we should just split uuuup!' She burst into fresh sobs.

'Oh, no, Erin, I'm so sorry,' Sophie said, sitting down next to her. Katy passed Erin fresh tissues. The others stroked Erin's hair and patted her arm gently.

'I just don't know what to do to make it work,' Erin sniffed.

'Maybe you just need to find things in common. It *is* easier if you have the same interests,' Kaz said. She looked around at the others for confirmation. 'Like me and Oliver being into the Grease Monkeys.'

'It's true, but then again differences can make a relationship stronger,' Katy chipped in. She shrugged.
'Opposites attract – that's what they say.'

Sophie knew Katy was talking about herself and
Callum, but she couldn't help thinking of her mum
and dad.

'Katy's right,' Sophie said. 'Maybe it's worth trying
to make it work. If you love each other enough. Trying
to get into the stuff he's into, that kind of thing. I
mean, he'd have to make the same effort for you too,
of course.' An image of Mark following Erin around
the village on one of her marathon shopping sprees
flitted into her head, and she couldn't help feeling a bit
doubtful.

Erin sniffed. 'Yeah, but having a boyfriend is meant
to be fun. I didn't think relationships were hard
work!'

Sophie sighed. Maybe Erin was right. Maybe love
wasn't the cure for everything after all – it certainly
didn't seem to be for Erin and Mark. She gazed at the
window. If love really wasn't always enough, what
about her plan to get Angelica and Robert back

together? *Maybe Dad's right,* she thought with a sinking feeling. *Maybe it wasn't such a good plan after all.*

The next morning, Sophie was up bright and early. Downstairs, she heard her mother on the phone. 'Yes ... no ... it can't be helped ... it's terribly inconvenient but I understand ... Goodbye.'

Sophie walked downstairs and her mother looked up at her.

'What's up, Mum? You look stressed.'

'Oh, it's one thing after another!' Her mum rubbed her forehead. 'The campsite in Holland just phoned. They've found suspicious blue-green algae in the swimming pool and they're closed till they can get it tested.'

Sophie didn't dare smile, but inside, she thought *Yes!* The spell had worked.

'So now I have to find an alternative venue,' her mother went on, leafing through the papers in her hands, 'and everything seems to be booked up.' She shook her head. 'I hope we won't have to cancel the whole thing.'

'I've got an idea,' said Sophie. She opened her bag and drew out a book called *Beautiful Jersey* – phase two of the plan. 'I borrowed this from the library the other day,' she said. 'For Geography,' she hastily added, 'but it actually looks really good. Maybe we could go to Jersey instead?' Her mother took the book. 'Honestly, Mum, it looks brilliant. There are miles and miles of coast paths for walking, and it would be perfect for orienteering. And there are loads of great activities to do, including the Durrell Wildlife Conservation Trust, and squillions of castles and things.'

'Jersey?' Her mother stared at the brochure. 'Well, that's certainly an idea.' Her face cleared as she turned the pages. 'It's a long time since I've been there, but yes, it certainly was special . . . ' She looked up, smiling. 'Thanks, Sophie. I'll look into it.'

As she walked away, Sophie did a quiet little dance of joy. She couldn't wait to tell Katy the spell had worked.

TEN

Sophie only allowed herself a one-hour lie-in the following Saturday. She glanced up at the sky. Could she and Katy manage to get their patches at Bowden Hospital perfect in a single day? If they did, would Mrs Freeman even let them go on the Gold Award trip next weekend? And although she'd dropped as many hints as she dared, her mother hadn't said for definite if they were going to Jersey or not.

A lot of things had to come together to make this work. But they had to try, at least.

She raced off to the school gates. As she reached them, she saw Katy – and then did a double take. Katy wasn't alone. She was followed by Erin, and Lauren, and Joanna and Kaz!

'Our patches could do with some more work too!' Erin said with a grin. 'I think maybe we were too busy gossiping ... '

Sophie laughed. It was going to be a lot more fun with six than with two!

When they arrived at the hospital, they got straight to work. Sophie weeded and dug and hoed and planted. After an hour, she leaned on her spade and, wiping the sweat from her eyes, looked back over the furrows she'd made. Her patch was really coming into shape – she had turned over and manured all the earth, and there wasn't a single weed to be seen. A robin hopped around a few feet away and, next to it, Gally, looking innocent, was slyly planting a few seeds as he scampered around on the turned earth.

Sophie turned and looked around at the rest of the garden. Katy's patch looked good too: she had put up bamboo canes for runner beans, and was carefully planting rows of rhubarb.

She glanced up towards the hospital. She'd wondered if she might see Robert Lloyd, but hadn't seen him yet. Maybe he'd already left for Jersey. She hoped so. If anyone could persuade Angelica not to wreak vengeance, it was he.

'How's it going, girls?' she called across the allotment to her friends.

'Pretty good!' Lauren said.

Erin looked up, her cheeks pink. 'Y'know what? This outdoors stuff is quite fun when you get into it.'

'Yoo-hoo, gardeners!'

Sophie heard a shout from the hospital, and looked up to see Sumira waving at them. 'Hot chocolate!' Sumira called, raising a mug towards them.

'Oh, yes!' Kaz dropped her spade and raced off. The others followed, stopping to put their things away tidily.

Sophie let them go on ahead. They'd worked hard, but she wasn't leaving a thing to chance. She dropped to her knees on the ground and chanted quietly,

'Forces of the Earth, earth, water, wind and fire ...
Please help me make the garden rich and beautiful!'

Magic tingled up her arms, as if a force were moving
through her. A gust of wind swept across the garden,
and the soil rippled like the sea, turning itself into neat
furrows. Under her feet, the earth trembled, and
stones came pushing up through the ground. Sophie
carried them away to the edges of the garden.

In the chestnut tree above, Gally sat up straight and
stared, then raced to join in. He got a handful of seeds
and ran up and down the furrows, tail whisking as he
stopped to plant each one. The earth covered them up
at once.

'Amazing!' Sophie smiled.

She beckoned Gally over to Katy's patch. The weeds
shrivelled up as soon as she touched them, and string
knotted itself together, pulling the beanpoles upright.

As soon as Katy's patch was looking as good as her
own, she dusted off her hands and headed back,
thirsty for some well-earned hot chocolate.

Her friends were sitting on the step by the hospital
doors, clutching steaming mugs. As she got nearer, she

heard Erin saying sadly, 'I don't think my patch is ever going to be right. I'm just not all that good at gardening.'

Sophie stopped. It was risky casting a spell on the others' patches, but Erin had been such a great help, so she wanted to help her, too.

She raced back down the path with Gally, and went over onto Erin's patch of ground.

'Forces of the Earth,' she repeated, touching her Source to the soil, 'make this garden neat!'

Again, the weeds shrivelled up, and Sophie ferried them to the compost heap. When she turned back to Erin's patch, it looked as if they'd spent hours working on it. Gally ran up and down, planting daffodil bulbs along the edges.

'Gardening would be a lot easier if it was always like this,' Sophie said to herself as she walked back to her own patch. But she had to admit that she actually liked it being hard – it was more fun eating a vegetable when it felt as if you'd really earned it!

'Impressive work, Sophie!' a voice said behind her.

Sophie gasped and turned around. 'Mrs Freeman! Where did you come from?'

'From school, of course.' Mrs Freeman, in her wellingtons, strode around the allotment, examining the different patches. 'The receptionist from the hospital called me; she was very impressed you had all chosen to spend a weekend working on the garden.'

Sophie watched her anxiously. She'd meant to tell Mrs Freeman what they'd done, but not until she was sure they had made their patches absolutely perfect. Mrs Freeman strode up and down, nodding as she passed each one. As she came to the end, she fixed Sophie with a keen look.

'You've worked hard,' was all she said.

Did that mean that they could go on the Gold Award trip? Sophie needed this more than anything, as then maybe she could save Katy's family. And save her own family, too.

Sophie gently pushed open the door to her grandmother's room. She was lying as still as ever in her hospital bed. Sophie tiptoed over and looked down at her pale face.

'Hello, Grandma,' she whispered.

Her grandmother gazed sightlessly up at the ceiling. Not a muscle twitched as the machines that monitored her heart beeped softly in the background.

Gally nuzzled up to Grandma's cheek while Sophie stroked her arm.

'Grandma, I don't know if you can hear me,' she went on, softly. 'But it's going to be OK. I'll sort everything out. I'll find a way to lift the curse.' She brightened. 'And Corvis is fine, too. He's at the vet and doing really well.'

She glanced at the door to check no one was listening, then bent and whispered in her grandmother's ear. 'Angelica's gone to Jersey. She means to destroy the thirteen chief witch hunter families with a terrible spell.' She took a deep breath. It made her nervous to think about it. 'And Dad's disappeared again. I think he's looking for her.'

The beeping from the machine sped up and it frightened Sophie.

'You mustn't worry,' she went on. 'Katy and I are going to go after them, and we'll make sure nothing bad happens.'

Although her grandma was motionless, Sophie could tell that she was trying to move.

'I promise everything will be all right. We have to do something to stop Angelica. The Thirteen Families may be witch hunters, but we can't let her do this to them.'

Sophie knew what they were about to do was dangerous, but the terror that suddenly appeared in her grandmother's eyes made her more scared than ever.

ELEVEN

'Before you skip off to classes,' Mrs Freeman said, smiling around at the crowded common room of Year 9 and Year 10 students, 'I wanted to let you know how very impressed I am with your hard work and dedication throughout the award. I'm delighted to say that every one of you has passed, and every one of you will be able to go on the Gold Award trip!'

Sophie squealed, but she could hardly hear herself over the cheering that had broken out. She punched the air, then turned and hugged Katy tightly.

'We did it, Katy!' she whispered in her ear.

'*You* did it!' Katy whispered back, grinning. 'Thanks, Sophie!'

As she drew back, Sophie spotted Callum and Mark at the other side of the room, their mouths open in disbelief. Sophie giggled. Arms behind her grabbed her and hugged her, and she turned round to see Erin's laughing face.

'Thanks, Sophie! I couldn't have done it without you! And I know I can get Mark back now,' Erin added in a whisper.

Callum came over and smiled sheepishly at Katy. 'Thanks, Katy,' he said. 'I don't know how you did it but I'm glad you did. But why didn't you call me? I would have helped!' He put an arm around her.

Katy smiled. 'No need. I'm sorry I left you in the lurch, Callum. I wanted to make it up to you.' Then, to Sophie's delight, she stood on tiptoes and kissed him.

Callum turned so red that Sophie couldn't help laughing, though it was a bit weird seeing her friends in a PDA.

'I'll leave you two to it!' Telling herself she was silly

to feel like a spare part, she backed away through the crowd ... and bumped into a firm chest. She turned round, ready to apologise, but her smile disappeared as she found herself face to face with Ashton.

'Funny how the garden got fixed so quickly,' Ashton said, raising a dark eyebrow. 'Almost as if by *magic*.' He grinned.

Sophie swallowed. *Maybe I went a bit too far*, she thought. If anyone else got suspicious ...

She tried to walk past Ashton, but he casually moved to block her way.

'Not talking to me? Shame,' he said, his eyes glittering. 'Well, we'll have the whole of the Gold Award trip to get to know each other better, won't we?'

Sophie rolled her eyes and pushed past him, but she didn't feel as confident as she tried to look. She could have kicked herself for not realising that fixing the garden meant Ashton would be going on the Gold Award trip as well.

'Students!'

Sophie stopped as Mrs Freeman's voice cut through the noise. She turned around.

'Before you go, I forgot to announce one pleasant and important detail. You all worked so hard that we decided to hold a prize draw for a dinner at Pizza Roma in the village. Katy Gibson and Callum Pearce were the winning pair.' She sighed as the common room broke out in wolf whistles.

First date! Sophie mouthed across the room.

Katy blushed and smiled back.

'And the hospital where we helped in their grounds called and said they would like to give another prize, also of dinner at Pizza Roma, to the pupils who made their favourite patch of garden. That goes to,' Mrs Freeman paused, 'Ashton Gibson and Sophie Morrow. Give them a round of applause, please!'

Sophie's smile vanished, replaced by a look of horror. She blushed as applause – and more wolf whistles – rang out.

'Speech! Speech!' called Kaz.

Luckily Sophie didn't have to answer, because at that moment her mum pushed the door of the common room open. The noise died down at once.

'Mrs Freeman? If you don't mind, I'd like to have a

quick word with the Gold Award students, about the changes to the trip.'

'Yes, of course.' Mrs Freeman nodded.

Sophie's mum waited for total silence, then went on: 'I'm very sorry to say that the trip to Holland has had to be cancelled.'

'No!' exclaimed Kaz. The other boys and girls groaned.

Sophie's mum raised her hand and waited for silence. 'But, don't worry: although we won't be going to Holland, we have managed to rearrange the trip. We found a great deal on an alternative campsite . . .'

This was it. Sophie crossed her fingers.

'. . . in Jersey.'

Sophie let out a whoop of delight – and Katy echoed it from the other side of the room. Sophie's mum grinned, and winked at Sophie. Sophie gave her a thumbs-up. Everything was going according to plan.

Pizza Roma was busy on Friday night, with couples and groups chatting and laughing in the candle-lit booths. Waiters rushed here and there, carrying giant pizzas. Sophie had been dreading the dinner all week and, now that she was here, she could only prod at her food with her fork. It looked and smelled delicious – but she couldn't work up an appetite with Ashton sitting opposite. Every time she bent her head to take a bite, she could feel his stare boring into her.

'How's your pizza, Katy?' Callum asked. He had a goofy, love-struck grin on his face as he gazed at Katy.

'Delicious!' Katy replied, beaming back at him. She seemed about to say something else, but Ashton cleared his throat. Katy caught his eye and her smile vanished.

Callum scowled at Ashton. Ashton eyeballed him back, picked up a bread-stick and snapped it in two. The sharp noise broke the tense silence like a balloon bursting, and made them all flinch.

Katy gave Callum a sad look.

Sophie pressed her lips together, wishing she could think of a spell to make Ashton disappear. She looked across the table for inspiration. A plate with salt, pepper, a bottle of chilli oil and parmesan stood there. As Ashton reached out for the chilli oil, she swiped it.

'Hey!' he protested.

'Sorry, there was something on the bottle.' Sophie turned away, pretending to dab at the bottle with a tissue. Instead, she rubbed her Source against it, murmuring, 'Forces of the Earth – earth, water, wind and fire, make this oil hotter than hot!' Then she turned round, smiling, and handed it back to Ashton. 'There you go – all clean!'

'Hmm,' Ashton said suspiciously. He up-ended the bottle and shook a few tiny drops onto his pizza, then took a bite. In a second his face turned red, then white. He spluttered and pushed back his chair, grabbing for his water. He missed and knocked his glass across the table; Sophie squealed as it tipped over her, soaking her dress.

'Ashton!' Katy shouted.

Ashton grabbed for another glass of water, and this time managed to glug it down, his eyes still watering.

'Sophie, are you OK?' Katy came round to dab at her dress.

'I'm soaked!' Sophie groaned. 'I'd better go back and change.'

It was her spell that had made the pizza so hot, but

she had been hoping it would make Ashton have to leave, not her!

'I'm off, too.' Ashton stood up with a final glare at Callum. 'This food is awful, and the company's even worse.' He flung down his napkin and stalked off to get his coat.

Sophie grinned at Katy and Callum. 'Bye, guys,' she said. At least they would be able to have a proper date now. It was worth a soaked dress for that.

'Sophie! Earth to Sophie!'

Sophie tugged her hat down over her ears, trying to shut out Ashton's voice. He'd been going on at her ever since they'd left the pizza restaurant, but she'd managed to block him out.

'Hey, *witch*!'

Sophie turned, startled by the anger in his voice. They were inside the school gates now, and she glanced around to check that no one crossing the courtyard had heard him. She speeded up her pace, but Ashton ran up behind her, grabbed her arm and spun her around.

'Let me go!' Sophie shook him off furiously.

'Then stop ignoring me!' Ashton shouted back.

Sophie stepped back in surprise.

Ashton took a deep breath. 'I can stand you being rude to me, teasing me, shouting at me, even burning the roof of my mouth off! But I can't stand you ignoring me!' he said, sounding like a sulky child. 'You're acting like I don't exist.'

I wish you didn't! Sophie thought. She spun on her heel and marched off towards the school without answering him.

Ashton caught up with her again, and blocked her path. Sophie tried to move around him, but he moved too.

'Get out of my way,' she snapped.

'No!' Ashton reached out and grabbed her shoulder. Then he leaned forwards. As his green eyes came towards her, Sophie suddenly remembered the night that they had almost kissed. Was he going to try and kiss her again?

She drew backwards, confused by the way she felt. She couldn't read the expression on Ashton's face, but the tight grasp of his hand on her shoulder made her knees feel weak.

He's a witch hunter, Sophie! she told herself furiously. *But then, so is Katy . . .* She'd always said they were not all bad.

As his lips moved towards hers, Sophie lifted her hand to push him away. For a second, she saw hurt in Ashton's eyes.

'I . . .' she began, not knowing what to say.

But suddenly Ashton wasn't looking at her. He was looking at her hand. Her Source glinted through the wool of her glove.

Ashton's hand slipped from her shoulder. With a sharp tug he pulled off her glove and the ring beneath it.

Sophie screamed as she felt her Source slide off her finger – it was as if her hair were suddenly yanked violently. What was more, it seemed to pull at her mind, too; as if part of her very self were being stolen. Ashton dropped her glove and raced towards the school, a dark shadow disappearing in among the other dark shadows.

'Forces of the Earth,' Sophie burst out, 'stop him!' She stretched out her hand, meaning to cast a spell on anything in reach, then stopped, staring at her bare hand. She couldn't cast magic without her Source!

She ran after Ashton, across the wet flagstones. Her heart hammered. She had hardly taken the ring off since she'd first found it; even in school, she had it round her neck on a chain. It felt as if part of herself had vanished, leaving a desperate, gaping hole. Panic rushed through her, and she suddenly realised how her demagicked grandmother must feel.

Ashton glanced back as he reached the main door.

'What's the matter, Sophie? Lost something?' he teased. He shouldered the main oak doors open and ran into the school.

Her lungs aching, Sophie chased after him, banging through the doors too. He rounded a corner and Sophie could no longer hear his footsteps. She was scared she might have lost him, but when she got round the corner she saw why he'd stopped.

Maggie Millar.

Maggie was rubbing her side, looking shocked, as

Ashton lay on the floor, apparently winded. The three of them gasped for breath in the sudden silence.

Maggie was the first to recover. She put her hands on her hips, a scowl darkening her face. 'Ashton Gibson!' she roared, and Ashton couldn't hide his look of fear. 'What are you doing running in the corridors? You could have really hurt me!'

'Maggie!' Sophie shouted. She felt tears bursting out of her eyes. 'Maggie, he stole my ring!'

Ashton tried to hide the ring in his pocket, but he was too late. Maggie's face hardened. She stepped forwards and held out her hand. 'Give that to me,' she said in a low voice.

For a second, Sophie thought Ashton might refuse. But he couldn't out-stare Maggie. Instead, he slowly handed her the ring and got to his feet, brushing himself down. He made as if to stroll past Maggie, but quick as a flash she grabbed him by the wrist.

'Not so fast!' Maggie looked down at the ring. Ashton squirmed and Maggie glared at him again, her face furious. 'Stealing!'

'I wasn't—'Ashton began.

'And bullying!' Maggie went on. Ashton opened his mouth and closed it again. He had turned red. 'This kind of behaviour is absolutely not tolerated at Turlingham. I shall be informing Mr Pearce, Mrs Morrow and Mrs Freeman.'

'Whatever,' Ashton muttered.

Maggie dropped his wrist with a look of contempt. 'You may go,' she said. 'But I doubt you've heard the last of this.' She pointed towards the boys' dormitories.

Ashton turned and opened his mouth to say something to Sophie, then seemed to think better of it. He strode off down the corridor, slamming the door behind him.

Sophie held her breath, preparing herself for the worst, expecting Maggie to start shouting at her for running in the corridor. Her Source would be confiscated. She might never get it back.

But Maggie stepped forwards and held out Sophie's ring. 'This ring is very important to you,' she said. 'I've noticed that.'

Sophie looked at her in disbelief. The head prefect

smiled as Sophie took the ring. 'Th-thanks, Maggie,' she managed, a huge lump in her throat.

'No need to thank me. Although,' she added anxiously, as Sophie slid the ring back on her finger, 'you will remember not to wear it in school hours, I hope.'

Sophie gave a half-laugh, half-sob. It was reassuring that Maggie was still Maggie! 'I will remember. And thanks again, Maggie. I owe you one!'

She pressed her hand over the cool shape of her ring. She had come so close to losing it. For the first time Sophie realised exactly how much her Source meant to her. Maybe it wasn't as bad as being demagicked, but losing her ability to cast spells would be like losing her sight or her hearing.

Being a witch might come with complications and dangers, but Sophie knew now that she wouldn't want to be anything else.

TWELVE

'It's here!' Erin shouted as the coach pulled into the drive.

Sophie cheered along with the rest of the Gold Award group. They were standing with their rucksacks in front of the main door of the school, while the teachers ticked off the last things on their checklists.

'OK, girls and boys, no pushing! You'll all find a seat!' Mrs Freeman shouted as the coach drew to a halt and its doors hissed open. The driver looked out nervously as the students surged towards the bus.

Sophie put a hand on Katy's arm as she was about to follow the others. 'Are you sure you brought everything we'll need?' she said in a low voice.

Katy nodded and tapped her rucksack. 'Sleeping bag – check. Lip gloss – check. Witch hunter kit – check. It all weighs a ton!' She made a face, then smiled. 'Don't worry, Sophie. If Angelica and your dad are there, we'll find them.'

'Hey, Katy!' Sophie turned to see Callum running towards them, his rucksack bouncing on his back. He went straight to Katy, a big grin on his face, and kissed her on the cheek. 'Looking forward to it?'

'Definitely!' Katy grinned back at him. 'So long as it doesn't rain, I'm happy.'

'Well, if you need any help putting your tent up, I'm the man to call.'

As the three of them walked to the coach together, Sophie realised she hadn't seen one person: Ashton. 'Um, aren't we missing a certain someone?' she asked.

'You mean the Brother Grimm?' said Katy.

Callum grinned. 'Didn't you hear? Ashton's been

chucked off the trip for stealing your ring ... and suspended for a week!'

'I know he's my brother but he totally deserves it,' Katy added.

'Agreed!' Sophie felt so relieved. *One less thing to worry about,* she thought. 'I am never, ever going to complain about Maggie Millar again,' she laughed.

'Hey, look,' Callum added. 'He's over there.'

Sophie followed Callum's gaze and spotted Ashton, standing beneath a tree with his shoulders hunched and his hands in his pockets.

'OK, I know this makes me a bad person, but I *have* to go and gloat,' she said, grinning. She left Katy and Callum and went off across the grass towards Ashton.

'Hey, Ashton,' she greeted him, unable to hide her smile. 'I'm sorry you got chucked off the trip. I bet you were really looking forward to a *spell* away in the *magical* surroundings of Jersey.'

To her surprise, Ashton didn't snap back. Instead, he looked at his feet and said quietly, 'Sophie, I don't care about missing the trip, or being suspended.' He glanced up at her, and Sophie was taken aback by the serious intensity in his eyes. 'I'm ... I'm ...' His face twisted and he seemed to be forcing himself to speak. 'I'm sorry,' he finished.

Sophie stared at him, speechless.

Ashton scowled at the ground. 'Taking your ring was a step too far. I shouldn't have done it – I was just, well, really upset when you pulled away from me.'

Sophie could only manage an incredulous laugh. Ashton looked up, and Sophie was even more startled to see he looked hurt.

He glanced around and leaned towards her. 'Listen, Sophie,' he said in a fierce whisper. 'I don't care about proving you're a witch – I just wanted to spend some time with you. You're different from any other girl I've ever met. You're funny, and kind, and fun. You don't try to be anything that you're not. And you're just ... different.'

Sophie's mouth opened and closed as she tried to think of something to say. Ashton was such a good actor that if she didn't know him so well, and if he hadn't been so cruel to Katy in the past – she thought back to Ashton's bullying behaviour to make Katy help him find Turlingham's witch – and shown himself to be so two-faced, she would almost have been fooled.

'Yeah … good joke,' she said uncertainly, backing away.

'Sophie!' Sophie turned round and saw her mum shouting for her. Everyone was on board the coach except her. Relieved at the chance to escape, she ran back to join them.

As she climbed on board, she risked a last glance out of the window. Ashton was still standing under the tree, and he was looking straight at her. Sophie tore her eyes away and focused on heading towards her friends. She found a seat near Callum and Katy, and lifted her rucksack into the overhead shelf, smiling as Gally peeked down at her from the side pocket.

She decided not to even try and work it out; she was not going to let thoughts of Ashton spoil her trip, and there was no way she would believe he meant what he had said. It was just another one of his tricks.

The two-person tent was cosy and snug; there was just room for her and Katy's sleeping bags, top to toe.

Sophie unzipped her rucksack and let Gally scamper out.

Someone unzipped the tent from outside. Katy poked her head through, pink-cheeked.

'It *definitely* won't fall down. I put double tent pegs in each hole,' she said, tucking a strand of hair behind her ear. 'Shall we go and see the others?'

'Yes!' Sophie scrambled out of the tent and emerged, blinking, into the field. She looked around with a sigh of pleasure. It was cold, but a beautiful evening, with the sun sinking red on the horizon and the evening star coming out. The cows in the next field were mooing away, and the tall trees at the edge of the campsite rustled in the gentle evening breeze.

Sophie and Katy walked over to their friends' tents, which were pitched not far away. They heard Erin's voice before they saw her, and grinned at each other.

'Knock, knock,' Sophie called outside the tent.

Joanna looked up through the tent flaps. 'Oh! You made me jump. I thought you were Mrs Freeman.' She giggled as they scrambled into the tent. She had a tin of biscuits in front of her; Erin and Lauren were inside too, munching away.

'This is cosy!' Sophie said, sitting down and hugging her knees. The tent just fitted the five girls.

'I smelled Jo's mum's famous cookies all the way from my tent, so I came over here to help her, um, sort them.' Erin said, grinning, her mouth full.

'We've got twenty, so will that be enough for a midnight feast?' Jo asked.

'Mm! Definitely. I've got some chocolates left over from half term,' Katy said.

Lauren added, 'Mum let me bring a packet of Jammy Dodgers.'

'Anyway, girls, I've got an amazing plan,' said Erin, popping the last crumb of her biscuit into her mouth. 'I've worked out how to make Mark fall back in love with me.' She beckoned them closer to her. 'See, the thing with boys is they're basically like dogs—' The others fell about in giggles, and Erin protested, 'No, listen! Boys want to feel useful, like they're saving you from things. Y'know, like in *Titanic*. So I'm going to ask Mark to help me put my tent up.'

'But, Erin,' said Lauren, 'our tent's already up!'

Erin grinned at them. 'I know,' she said, and headed for the exit.

Sophie, Katy, Lauren and Joanna stuck their heads out to see Erin walking towards her own tent, brushing the crumbs from her hands.

She walked around it and pulled out the poles. The tent collapsed on itself like a deflating balloon. Lauren gasped.

'Heeelp ... please!' Erin glanced around, and aimed her cries at Mark's tent. 'My tent's fallen down!' She bent down and pulled out a few tent pegs.

Sophie spluttered with laughter. On the other side of the campsite, Mark popped up like a meerkat and swivelled around to see what was happening.

'Are you OK, Erin?' he asked.

'Nooooo,' Erin wailed. 'I can't do this!'

Mark jumped up and came quickly over.

'Come on – let's get out of their way!' Sophie beckoned to the others, and they ran off, giggling, down the sloping field towards the trees.

'I can't believe she did that,' Lauren said, frowning,

as they got to the trees. 'It took us for ever to get the tent up!'

'Never mind, Lauren,' Sophie laughed. 'Mark will have it up again in no time, I bet. Hang on,' she added, as they slowed down, 'where's Kaz?'

'Good question!' Jo looked surprised. 'She went off with Oliver to get firewood, but that was ages ago.'

Sophie led the way into the woods, calling Kaz's name. She hadn't gone far into the trees when she spotted something bright orange: Kaz's jacket, by the trunk of a pine tree.

'Kaz!' She headed towards it, and skidded to a halt, her eyes wide.

It was Kaz, all right. And she wasn't alone. She was with Oliver and they were holding hands, gazing deep into each other's eyes. Almost as if they were about to kiss!

Sophie gasped, Lauren and Jo squealed, and Katy trod on a branch that cracked loudly. Sophie turned round and, herding her giggling friends in front of her, ran back out of the woods.

'This is a great school trip so far!' Jo said with a laugh as they reached the campsite again.

'Totally,' Lauren giggled.

But Sophie had to remember that for her and Katy, it wasn't just a school trip. They had serious work to do.

Sophie lay in the tent, reading by torchlight, but it was hard to concentrate on her book. It was almost eleven, and Katy had sneaked out to see Callum. Sophie couldn't help listening for her coming back. If she got caught, she'd be in big trouble. And if Katy got sent back to school in disgrace, Sophie would be left without her best friend for the rest of the week – a spare part again.

I'm so selfish! she scolded herself. Her two best friends were together and she was really pleased about that, so why was she minding so much about being left on her own? Maybe it was because of Ashton. She couldn't stop thinking about what he'd said to her, and she wished she could talk to her best friends about it – but she couldn't talk to either of them as they were too wrapped up in each other!

She blinked as a bright beam of torchlight came in through the tent flaps. Then she heard someone crying. Sophie sat up quickly, shielding her eyes against the torchlight. 'Hello?'

'Oh, Sophie!' It was Katy. She switched off the torch and Sophie heard her sobbing as she collapsed on her sleeping bag.

'What happened? Katy?' Sophie moved over and put an arm around her.

'It's C-C-Cal—'

'Callum? Oh, no,' she said, as Katy nodded against her shoulder. 'What happened?' She spotted a packet of tissues and passed them to Katy.

Katy sat back and blew her nose. She went on, hiccupping back sobs. 'We ... had a conversation ... and he said ... he tried to get me a present ... a hardback of the book ... the one about witches ... '

Sophie could guess what Katy was going to say next. 'And he found out it didn't exist!' she finished for her.

Katy nodded. 'He said I was hiding things from him,' she went on. 'And he's right. I hate it, but he's right.' Katy sniffed. 'Then he asked what I was really talking about that time in the common room . . . and when I wouldn't tell him . . . he said I didn't trust him.'

'Oh, no!'

'He broke up with me!' Katy burst into a fresh storm of sobs, and Sophie hugged her tightly.

'Maybe,' Sophie began, not really believing what she was saying but feeling as if she had to try, 'maybe you can fix it. Maybe there's some way . . . he can't mean it.'

Katy shook her head. 'How, Sophie? I can't possibly tell him the truth. And he deserves a girlfriend who can be honest with him.'

Sophie had no answer. Despite sometimes feeling left out, she wished more than anything she could help Katy stay with Callum . . . and not just because her best friend was so upset. Katy and Callum were so much like her mum and dad. If her friends couldn't work things out, what hope was there for her family?

THIRTEEN

As Sophie hiked along the narrow cliff path with her friends, she couldn't help wondering why Erin hadn't said a word about getting back together with Mark. Erin was striding off at the front, pausing now and then to check the map and compass. Behind her, the rest of them – Sophie, Katy, Joanna, Kaz and Lauren – straggled along the path, turning to chat to one another as they walked. Bringing up the rear, and trying to go unnoticed, was Gally, who scampered along the rocks like an acrobat.

'I just don't get it,' Lauren said to Katy. 'You and Callum were so good for each other.'

'He's mad!' Kaz declared, putting an arm around Katy.

Katy swallowed. 'Girls, you're so lovely, but I don't want to talk about it. It's too upsetting.'

The others made sympathetic noises. Kaz squeezed Katy's shoulder.

'Let's talk about happier things.' Katy raised her voice. 'Erin! Aren't you going to tell us all about getting back with Mark?'

Erin had the map open and was struggling to fold it up again. 'No,' she replied, firmly. 'We've got a job to do here, girls. Let's stop gossiping and get on with the orienteering task.'

Sophie's mouth dropped open and the others exchanged amazed glances.

'Hey, Erin, what's with the personality transplant?' Kaz asked.

'Yeah,' said Joanna. '*No gossiping?* Who *are* you?'

'I don't know what you mean,' Erin sniffed. 'But like Mark said, outdoor activities are fun, apparently. So we should try and find the points on the list, and do it really fast so we beat the boys!' She scowled at the map. 'Can anyone work out where we are on this thing? And can someone make it fold up again? It's just, like, possessed.'

Sophie laughed, and Katy laughed too. Sophie hung the compass around her neck and looked at the map of Jersey Erin was holding. 'OK, so, it's upside down,' she pointed out. 'If you hold it this way up, north-north-west is here, and—'

Erin yawned, and everyone burst out laughing.

'OK, I tried,' Erin said, shaking her head. 'I can't take this orienteering stuff any more. I *need* to gossip!' She tossed the map in the air, and Sophie caught it. 'I'm so thrilled to be back with Mark, it's just the best thing ever! But Katy, what is Callum *thinking*? He must be nuts! And Kaz, what happened with you and Oliver? Did you kiss, or what?'

Erin babbled on about her and Mark, Katy and Callum, Kaz and Oliver, as they descended the cliff path. Looking up, Sophie spotted Mr Powell's bright blue jacket; he was standing on a little wooden jetty that stuck out into the sea. At the beach end of it was a wooden boathouse that had once been painted pink but was now worn to a greyish sort of rose colour. The beach stretched away, empty as far as the eye could see.

'Mr Powell!' Sophie waved, and they rushed up to him.

'You made it! *Precisely* on time. Well done, girls.' Mr Powell made a note on his clipboard. 'OK, here's your next grid reference.' He handed them a card. 'Mrs Freeman will be waiting for you there.'

Sophie turned as she heard Katy gasp. Mr Powell looked up.

'Something wrong, Katy?'

'Oh, no . . . just . . . nothing!' But Katy looked pink and excited. As soon as Mr Powell turned his back, she whispered to Sophie: 'I saw a cat sneaking behind the boathouse, and I'm sure it was a Siamese!'

'Mincing?' Sophie asked, and looked at the boat-house. If Katy was right and the cat was Angelica's familiar, she could be very close. They'd have to investigate. But not while Mr Powell was standing right there.

The others carried on and Sophie and Katy had to run to catch up with them.

The wind blew straight in from the water as the girls made their way back up the cliff path, and Sophie's hair whipped around her face. Skeins of mist, like grey ghosts, blew past them, clammy and cold when they touched their skin.

Sophie's mind was firmly back on witch business. She took Katy's arm and they fell behind the others. 'Do you know exactly where the witch hunter gathering is being held?' Sophie asked.

'Not yet,' Katy replied. 'I spoke to my parents and tried to find out. They got a bit suspicious, though, so I had to stop asking questions. All I know is that it's on one of the islands nearby.'

'Hmm.' Sophie shook her head. 'It's not enough. There are loads of little islands around Jersey. I'm worried, Katy. I mean, all these people in terrible danger – I know they're witch hunters and I'm supposed to hate them, but I wouldn't want anything bad to happen to anyone.'

'You and me both. We've got to think of a way to get

back to that boathouse later on,' Katy murmured under her breath. 'I'm pretty sure that was Mincing I saw. Which means Angelica's near by.'

Sophie nodded. Mist drifted along from the sea, and for a moment she couldn't see her friends.

'Maybe if we sneak off after supper?' Katy suggested.

'We'll still be spotted. It has to be when everyone's—'

'Hey, girls! Are you OK back there?' Kaz called, looking back at them through the mist.

'Just checking the map,' Sophie said, quickly beginning to unfold it.

As she did so, she spotted a figure in a dark coat walking towards them along the path. The fog clouds cut in between them and Sophie tried to make out the person's face as she heard the footsteps crunch past without pausing.

She was about to fold up the map again when Erin shrieked, 'It's Jareth Quinn!'

'What? Where?' Joanna, Kaz and Lauren spun round.

'Right there!' Erin was pointing after the person who had just passed them.

Sophie laughed. 'Good joke, Erin! What would a movie star like Jareth Quinn be doing on top of a cliff in Jersey?'

Joanna ran towards them and a little way down the path, staring after the figure.

'It's not Jareth Quinn,' she burst out. 'It's Ashton Gibson!'

Sophie stared down the path, remembering how Erin had thought she had spotted heart-throb actor Jareth Quinn when she had first seen Ashton Gibson.

The figure had disappeared into the fog. She gave Katy a shocked look.

'How can Ashton be here? He's been suspended,' Kaz said. 'Katy?'

Katy had turned white. 'Of course,' she mumbled. 'My-my parents were planning a short break in Jersey. They must have taken him with them.' She looked meaningfully at Sophie.

To the witch hunter gathering! thought Sophie,

getting Katy's unspoken message. But if it *was* him, then he was in danger, too.

Sophie realised with a shock that she was actually afraid for Ashton Gibson. Angelica would obliterate him with the rest of the witch hunters. Unless someone stopped her.

FOURTEEN

Sophie led the way on tiptoe, moonlight lighting their way across the rocks towards the shadowy hulk of the boathouse. Now and then she and Katy stopped to steady themselves as they came to a slippery patch of seaweed. They had been using Sophie's torch up until then, but on nearing the boathouse had decided to rely on the moon instead.

It had been hard to get away from the campsite; they had stopped and held their breath at every twig that cracked underfoot. Luckily, everyone had been exhausted from their hike the day before, and Sophie could hear them all breathing heavily through their tents.

Now she listened hard, but the rush of the waves on the beach seemed to blot out any other sound. The moon cut a long track across the sea, and she could make out the white line of the surf pushing in and pulling back.

She hesitated. 'I wonder if this really is where Robert and Angelica are hiding,' she whispered to Katy.

'There's only one way to find out,' Katy whispered. 'Let the Bloodhound sniff them out.'

She reached up to her neck and Sophie saw her draw out a silver chain. A needle-like metal bar dangled on the end of it – The Witch Hunters' Bloodhound. Sophie automatically rubbed the back of her hand. She still had a scar there from where the Bloodhound had caught her once.

'Did you bring the compass?' she whispered back.

Katy handed it over. As long as the magnet inside

the compass was blocking Sophie's powers, the Bloodhound wouldn't point towards her.

Katy dangled the Bloodhound pendant in front of herself. At once the needle began twisting in the air, as if it was looking for something. Sophie watched, feeling a shiver down her spine as the needle, glinting in the moonlight, swung back and forth. Then it pulled towards the boathouse.

Katy was showing the effort as she held the chain. 'It feels really strong,' she whispered as she moved towards the boathouse. 'As if there's more than one witch here.'

They reached the boathouse and flattened themselves against the wall as Katy placed the Bloodhound back around her neck. As silently as they could, they edged to the corner and peered around to the side of the boathouse.

Sophie saw the square of light from the window at once. She beckoned Katy after her. They made their way to the window and peered over the sill.

Sophie saw Angelica. Then she saw Robert Lloyd. They'd found them! Maybe Robert had convinced

Angelica not to do anything, and Sophie and Katy's job was already done.

Angelica was sitting at the far end of the boathouse, on a wooden bench. On the walls hung the dark shapes of dinghies and sea kayaks, fastened to racks. A few candles stood here and there, casting almost as much shadow as they did light. Robert sat next to her. They seemed to be arguing, Robert gesturing wildly, and Angelica shaking her head.

'Can you hear what they're fighting about?' Katy asked, in a whisper.

Sophie shook her head.

Along the wall she saw a door. She beckoned to Katy, and they edged along until they reached it. Sophie reached out and pushed it so it was ajar. At once she heard the clamour of voices. Angelica and Robert were speaking together and, as she listened, a familiar voice rose above them.

Her dad! He was here, in Jersey!

'He must have trusted your witch hunter ritual after all!' Sophie whispered to Katy.

Wide-eyed, Katy nodded to show she'd heard.

'Listen to what I have to say, please!' Sophie's dad shouted. Putting her eye to the crack of the door, Sophie could see her father from this angle. He was pacing up and down, speaking passionately.

'I understand your anger against the witch hunters. But this Obliteration spell you want to cast is evil; it will make you no better than them,' he said. 'Besides, not all the witch hunters are here on Jersey, and once the others have found out what you have done to their leading families, they won't stop hunting you until you're dead.'

'But we don't want to attack the Gathering,' Robert told him. 'That's what I was trying to tell you. I've spoken to Angelica. I've persuaded her it was a foolish idea.'

Sophie's dad's head shot up, and he looked hopeful.

Sophie grinned at Katy. She knew she'd been right to trust in the power of love!

'We have a new plan now,' Robert added, and Sophie's heart sank a little.

'A new plan?' Sophie's father sounded suspicious.

'Yes, and you'll like it. We're going to reason with

them, bargain with them.' He looked at Angelica affectionately. 'We don't want anyone to be hurt unnecessarily.'

'All we want is to live in peace, together,' Angelica agreed. 'Now that we're back together, we see everything so clearly. We're so much stronger as a couple than we ever were apart.'

Katy raised her hand, and she and Sophie tapped their hands together in a silent high five. Sophie could hardly stop herself doing a little dance of happiness.

She turned back to the door. Her father was staring at Robert, looking dumbfounded. Then a smile slowly spread over his face. 'Well, I'm delighted! I'll admit it, I was wrong, Robert.' He stepped forwards, holding out his hand. 'I hope you'll forgive my hasty judgement and shake hands with me.'

Robert got to his feet, smiling, and Sophie pushed the door open, ready to break into a run and hug her father.

But then she saw the stone necklace in Robert's other hand.

Robert clasped her father's hand in his own and

quickly flung the necklace over his wrist. While Sophie's dad looked down in astonishment, Angelica chanted: 'Blood and bone, turn to stone! Cold and old and still as earth, I curse the one who shared my birth!'

The chain seemed to melt away and disappear. Sophie's dad became still, trapped like a fly in amber.

'It's done!' Robert sounded almost frightened. 'The book is more powerful than I ever imagined. I would never have guessed the Spell of Stone was so strong.'

Angelica ignored him. A terrible smile came over her face as she looked at her brother. 'Yes, violence is foolish,' she said sweetly. 'It's much better to strike a bargain. And now we have the perfect bargaining chip.' She put out a finger and prodded Sophie's father in the chest. Franklin swayed, but didn't move. 'You!'

'Dad!' Sophie screamed, and took a few steps forward – she couldn't help it. But her voice died in her throat as Robert's gaze snapped towards her.

'Sophie,' growled Angelica, scowling. She snapped her fingers at Franklin. 'Walk!' she commanded.

Robert held Franklin's wrist in a tight grip and

pulled him away. He stumbled after Robert like a puppet being dragged across the floor, his eyes furious and shocked as the spell stopped him from controlling his movement.

'What are you doing?' Sophie's voice broke.

'Cousin Robert!' Katy was beside her. 'Can't you see Angelica's plan is evil?'

Robert didn't even look at her, his gaze turned adoringly towards Angelica. 'Sorry, kids, but I love her – nothing she does can be wrong.'

Angelica moved towards the far side of the boat-house, holding a torch. 'This way, Robert! The side door!' she shouted.

A boat hung above the door. Sophie thought fast. If she could make the wires that held up the boat dissolve ... She dropped the compass so the magnet no longer touched her skin.

'Forces of the Earth!' she cried out, holding up her hands, 'earth, water, wind and fire: let salt water rust the metal!'

The air shuddered and her Source glowed white. There was a rumble, then a crumbling shower of red rust fell from the back wall as Angelica and Robert ran towards it, Robert still dragging Sophie's dad by the wrist. The boat crashed down, blocking their path.

Angelica spun around. 'Clever,' she said, her eyes glinting. 'But you stay away from us, or you'll regret it!'

'No!' shouted Katy.

Sophie begged, 'No, please! He's your brother, Angelica – you can't do this!'

Angelica cackled, and Sophie shuddered as she saw the mixture of love and madness in her eyes as she turned to Robert. 'I have Robert now. He's my whole family,' she answered. 'Now get out of our way!'

Sophie tried to grab hold of her dad as Robert forced him towards the main door, but the force of the spell kept him moving, pulling him from her grasp. Angelica pushed past the girls and followed Robert towards the water, wading into it. For a second Sophie didn't know what they would do; then she spotted the motorboat bobbing just off-shore.

Robert forced her dad – still in a trance – into the boat. Angelica scrambled after them.

With a burst of petrol fumes the engine roared into

life. It sped away into the darkness, leaving a wake of white water behind it, glowing in the moonlight.

Sophie stared after it in horrified terror. Her father was trapped, just like her grandma ... and headed straight for the witch hunters!

FIFTEEN

'Dad!' Sophie screamed. She ran into the water, stumbling as the cold waves quickly numbed her legs. But the boat was gone. All Sophie could see, her eyes straining desperately against the dark, was the faint, distant beam of a lighthouse, coming and going as it swept a semicircle of light across the water. The sound of the motorboat faded away and finally vanished completely.

Sophie's heart pounded. 'We've got to do something!'

Katy looked around, and then pointed at the boat-house. 'In there. I saw a dinghy.'

Katy turned and ran to the boathouse. She flung open the door and clattered in with Sophie right behind her. Katy pushed the boats and oars aside, and tugged out a small white boat.

'You mean you know how to sail?' Sophie's heart leaped.

'Not exactly,' Katy said, as they pushed the boat out onto the beach. 'But we've got to try *something*!'

The boat scraped across the pebbles and bobbed out into the water. Sophie picked up the compass and then waded out to the boat. She was about to get in when she heard stones clack against each other on the shore. She turned round, steadying herself as the boat bobbed up and down.

Katy, still on the beach, looked startled. 'What was that?'

They stared into the darkness.

Sophie started as she heard running footsteps coming along the beach, thudding on the sand and kicking pebbles aside.

There was another rattle of stones falling and Sophie gasped as she saw a tall, messy-haired shadow step out of the darkness.

'Callum!' said Katy, just as Sophie recognised him. 'What are you doing here?'

Callum stared at them, and Sophie's smile disappeared as she saw the shock in his eyes.

'I saw you sneaking out of your tent so I followed you. What's going on? Are you seriously trying to steal a *boat*?'

'I . . . I . . . ' Katy stuttered.

Sophie broke in. 'Callum, I'm so sorry, we can't explain. We just . . . we have to go. It's urgent.'

'You're going out to sea in that tiny thing, in the middle of the night? Are you mad?' Callum stepped forwards.

'Please, Callum,' Sophie begged. 'Can't you just trust me? We're friends, right?'

Callum shook his head slowly, looking uncertain. 'Sophie, of course we're friends, but—'

'Callum, please.' Sophie begged. 'It's my dad.'

Katy nodded.

'Are you guys serious?' Callum looked back and forth between them. 'There really is something important going on, isn't there?'

'Yes. Something terrible; and it's my fault!' Sophie's voice broke. If she and Katy hadn't found out Angelica was in Jersey, her dad wouldn't even be there. If she hadn't trusted Robert, her father wouldn't be in such awful danger. She'd thought Robert would be a good influence on Angelica – but it had turned out that she was a bad influence on him!

Katy ran forwards and took Callum's hands, squeezing them tight. 'Callum,' she said in a low, desperate voice. 'We have to go. But when I come back I'll tell you the truth. About everything. I promise.'

'No,' said Callum, firmly.

The girls stared at him in horror.

'You think I'm going to let you set sail in the middle of the night on your own? Do you even know *how* to sail?'

'Well . . . ' Sophie looked despairingly at Katy. Was Callum going to ruin everything?

'Because I do!' Sophie gaped as Callum stepped into

the boat. 'I'm coming with you to see that you don't drown yourselves. Come on!'

He held out a hand and Sophie took it and jumped into the boat, followed by Katy. Callum pulled on some ropes and the sail rose. The wind tugged at it, and Callum moved back and forth, securing some ropes and pulling on others. The boat pulled away, out to sea.

Sophie looked out into the darkness ahead, and told herself to be strong. *I'm coming, Dad.*

SIXTEEN

The boat moved silently through the dark sea and came to a stop, rocking on the waves, the only sound the slap of water against the hull. The beam of the lighthouse cut over their heads, sweeping the sea behind them. Sophie gazed at the shadowy island ahead of them. The boat had headed in this direction. Her father had to be here ... somewhere.

Katy brought out the Bloodhound.

Callum watched her and frowned. 'That's a funny sort of necklace. It looks dangerous.'

'It is,' Sophie said, taking hold of the compass again

so the magnet protected her. She looked at Katy. They would have to tell Callum the truth now. 'If you're a witch.'

Callum shook his head. 'What?'

Sophie chose to ignore him. There was no time to explain now.

'There!' Katy interrupted. The Bloodhound was pointing towards the dark line of the shore.

'It's all rocks in there. We could easily hit one.' Callum sounded doubtful.

'There must be a way in if they came this way,' Sophie said.

'OK,' Callum sighed. 'But we'll need to row.' He picked up the oars. 'The wind will just drive us onto the rocks, otherwise.'

They moved through the water, the only sound the clop of the oars in the sea. Katy, her eyes fixed on the Bloodhound, whispered directions to Callum. 'Just to the left ... now straight ahead ... '

Sophie looked down and saw they were passing over dark shadows, rocks that could tear a hole in the bottom of the boat.

'It's pulling!' Katy gasped. The needle drew away from them, so the chain was horizontal on the air, pointing towards the coastline.

As they got closer the dark cliffs rose above them, cutting out the moonlight so it was pitch-black. The beam of the lighthouse swept towards the shore. In its brief flash, Sophie saw that right in front of them was a dark shadow, tall and narrow: the entrance to a sea cave.

'There!' she whispered, pointing.

'I see it!' Callum was looking over his shoulder, and nodded.

The Bloodhound needle pointed directly into the black cave. As their boat drifted into it, Sophie gasped as she made out a dark shape in the water – the motorboat. Their own boat ground to a halt on the sandy bottom, next to it.

Sophie could feel her heart beating hard. Waves echoed and sloshed around her. Her torch picked out footprints in the wet sand, leading towards the back of the cave. The witch hunter magic had worked. They'd found them. Now all they had to do was see what was inside this cave ... and hope they could save her dad.

Katy led the way with the Bloodhound while Sophie shone the torch ahead of her, so she could see her way along the tunnel. Her feet crunched on seaweed and shells. The salt in the air stung her lips.

'I think now is a good time to tell me what's going on,' Callum began.

Sophie sighed and whispered: 'Callum, this isn't going to be easy for you to cope with.' She hesitated. 'What would you say if I told you witches are real?'

As she spoke, she heard another noise among the sounds of dripping water and the far-away boom of waves against rocks: voices.

She raised a hand as Callum began to speak. 'Listen! Can you hear that?'

Katy and Callum shook their heads.

'I think it's the witch hunters. We're on the right track.'

'I can't hear anything.' Callum looked at her in disbelief.

'I've got good hearing. It's because I'm . . . ' Again, she hesitated, suddenly scared of saying it aloud. What if Callum didn't accept it? What if he thought witches were evil, like she once had?

'The thing is, Callum,' said Katy nervously, 'I haven't been telling you everything.'

'I knew it,' Callum said, coming to a stop. He folded his arms across his chest. 'Go on,' he said, defensively, 'I can take it.'

'You see, I . . . I'm a witch hunter.' Katy stopped, looking anxiously into his face.

Callum was expressionless for a second. 'Say again?' he said finally.

'My whole family are.' Katy sighed. 'We're a group of people who hunt down witches and take away their magic. We've done it for centuries.'

'This is a pretty realistic dream,' said Callum, scratching his head quizzically. 'When do the elves come in?'

'It's not a dream, Callum!' Sophie broke in. 'Katy's telling the truth.'

'Uh-huh. That her family are . . . witch hunters.

Katy, I hate to break this to you, but there are no such things as witches.' Callum had started to walk on, sounding angry now. 'I thought you were going to be honest with me.'

Sophie could understand why Callum was angry. It was a lot to take in: it had taken her a while to believe the truth herself. 'She *is* being honest and witches *do* exist,' Sophie told him as she hurried after him. 'I know' – she took a deep breath – 'because I *am* one.'

'Look you two. I don't—' Callum started, but Sophie saw a light ahead and cut him off by putting her finger to her lips. The light was shining around a rock, flickering like candlelight, and the voices suddenly sounded sharper and louder.

She switched off her torch and crept along. When she reached the last boulder she pressed herself flat against it, edged forwards and peered around it.

She was looking into a huge cavern. Stalactites hung from the ceiling. Candles had been placed in clefts and on ledges all over, so that shadows danced and jumped here and there. The cavern was *full* of people.

'It's the Gathering!' Katy whispered behind her.

Sophie turned. Katy was shaking, and Callum's mouth hung open.

The witch hunters were sitting and standing in small groups around a central podium. There were men and women of all ages, and even some teenagers. All seemed to be in the middle of a discussion, their voices echoing from the walls of the cavern in a bouncing sea of noise. A tall woman ticked off numbers on her fingers as she talked to a short, fat man in a suit. 'Three of them ... evil creatures ... '

For the first time, Sophie really realised the danger she was in.

Another man with a high, squealing voice waved his arms and Sophie caught the occasional word: 'vermin ... need to demagick ... must be a concerted effort ... '

Katy leaned forwards, speaking in a low voice: 'It's all of the thirteen chief families!' Her gaze moved across the scene. 'The man with the red beard is one of the Pengelleys, and that fat man with the awful voice is head of the Stanley family. I can see lots of Carvers – they're really committed, all of them.'

'The thirteen chief families? *Witch* hunters?' Callum sounded stunned. 'You mean it's true, all that stuff you were saying?'

Katy turned to him and nodded.

'I didn't tell you because I-I didn't know how you'd react.' She licked her lips. 'Callum, I came to Turlingham to look for a witch. And I found one.' She looked at Sophie. 'But it didn't work out quite as planned.'

Sophie continued for her. 'You see, I'm a witch, and Katy's a witch hunter. But somehow, we're still best friends.'

Callum stared at them in silence.

'And those ... those people are witch hunters?' he asked, nodding towards the cavern. 'Those are your family, Katy?'

Katy nodded unhappily. 'So to speak.'

Callum looked into the cavern again. 'Katy! Your parents!' he whispered, and pointed.

Mr and Mrs Gibson stood, looking formal and stiff, in the middle of the group. There was someone else standing near them, too: a slim, tall figure in a suit.

Sophie glimpsed dark hair as the crowd moved back and forth, then as the figure half turned, she picked out the flash of familiar green eyes.

'Ashton ...' Sophie and Katy whispered it at the same time.

He *was* here! Ashton had come to the Gathering. Sophie was surprised by how disappointed she felt. She'd been hoping he wasn't as bad as she'd thought he was.

But Ashton looked very uncomfortable. In the midst of all the adults, he suddenly seemed young, and a lot less sure of himself. His familiar sneer was nowhere to be seen.

A grizzled man in an ill-fitting suit strode up to the podium and tapped on it several times with a gavel. The noise echoed around the room, and the witch hunters turned towards him, their conversation dying away.

'That's the Master of the Witch Hunt,' Katy whispered. 'He's kind of like a president.'

The man smiled, showing yellow, pointed teeth. Around his neck hung a strange chain, like a mayor's chain of office, but it seemed to be made of random pieces of jewellery, watches, hair slides, photographs and other little objects. It made a strange contrast with his formal appearance.

'That's a funny chain,' Sophie said, in a low voice.

'It's made of the stolen Sources of witches,' Katy whispered, sounding embarrassed.

Sophie was horrified. Her hand went automatically to cover her ring as she remembered the heartbreaking pain she'd felt when Ashton had stolen it.

'And now, dear friends, the part of the evening we have all been waiting for. This is a moment to celebrate our success, to share our scores with each other and spur each other onto new triumphs. Who will be first?'

Sophie looked at Katy questioningly, wondering what 'the scores' meant. Katy had a wary, queasy look on her face.

A young woman in an elegant blue dress strode forwards at once, nodding to friends in the audience.

'Elvira Carver,' the Master announced, and stepped back.

The woman took her place at the podium and beamed. 'I'm sure you all recall the hunt that my father and I were engaged on,' she announced, her voice clear as crystal. 'I'm delighted to tell you that it ended in success. Three demagicked and one stolen Source to add to my collection. A good end to the year!' She held up a battered-looking copper bracelet.

Sophie's mouth dropped open as the witch hunters burst into applause and shouted cheers. Those demagicked witches could have been her poor grandmother!

A man had replaced Elvira at the podium. 'I've demagicked five,' he announced, rubbing his hands together. 'Not a bad score!'

The cavern thundered with cheers.

How could they be so cruel? Sophie thought. *Witches are people, too!*

Katy felt for her hand and squeezed it protectively.

'And what about our younger members?' The Master stepped back to the podium, grinning again. 'I see fresh young faces here tonight, no doubt desperate to tell us of their successes. Anna Wythers?'

The crowd parted to reveal a lanky girl with a

slightly startled expression. She didn't look much older than Sophie herself.

'I demagicked my first witch this year!' she squeaked. 'I hope it's the first of many!'

The crowd roared approval.

'And what about Ashton Gibson?'

Sophie pressed a hand to her mouth. She didn't want to hear it. No matter how bad Ashton was, she couldn't bear to know how many witches he had tracked down and demagicked, or how close she'd come to being one of his victims.

The crowd parted, leaving Mr and Mrs Gibson looking uncomfortable, one on either side of Ashton, who was pale and sweating.

'I ... er ... I ...'

'Come along, Ashton!' The Master sucked his teeth in disapproval. 'When your parents informed me you would be attending the Gathering this year I presumed you had some achievements to announce.' He grinned and looked around for approval as the crowd chuckled. But when he looked back at Ashton he was frowning. 'Are you telling me that you have failed?'

Ashton hung his head.

'He's only just started at a new school,' Mrs Gibson said, turning pink. She put an arm around Ashton, but Ashton shrugged it off furiously. There were jeers and groans from the crowd.

'What kind of a witch hunter are you?' shouted a voice from the crowd.

Sophie spun round to Katy. 'I don't get it. Ashton acts so ruthless.'

Katy shrugged, and smiled without humour. 'Ashton's a rubbish witch hunter. Why do you think my parents bug *me* so much?'

'You ... you haven't—' Sophie stared at her, not wanting to say the horrible thought in her mind.

'No. I promise,' Katy said. 'I've found witches before now. I didn't understand it was wrong. But I've never demagicked one.' She shuddered, and added, looking pleadingly at Callum: 'And now, I never, ever would.'

Sophie squeezed her hand, and Callum managed a smile.

'You're a disgrace!' someone else in the crowd yelled to Ashton.

Ashton backed away, looking frightened.

'Good for nothing!'

'Call yourself a witch hunter?'

'Pathetic!'

The Master shook his head in disgust, then tapped his nails on the wood.

'I . . . I . . . I . . . no, wait! Listen!' Ashton shouted desperately. 'I have news: big news!' The crowd turned back to Ashton. 'I've found Angelica Poulter.'

There was a sudden, shocked silence. Sophie couldn't believe it. Ashton *had* been doing some of his own witch hunting, up there on the cliff!

'And that's not all.' Ashton's voice swelled with confidence. 'She wasn't alone. She was with Robert Lloyd. The traitor.'

'What?' exclaimed Mr Gibson.

Cries of shock and outrage went up from the rest of the witch hunters.

'They were near here,' Ashton went on. 'On Jersey. I saw both of them.' He looked around the crowd.

There was a muttering from everyone. Witch hunters turned to each other, disbelieving and doubtful.

'So why didn't you do something?' said the Master, staring straight at Ashton.

Ashton's eyes widened and he looked panicked. The witch hunters in front of him laughed. Sophie shuddered at the cruel sound.

'Yeah, kid, if you saw them so clearly, how come you didn't get rid of them?' shouted a fat woman.

Ashton opened his mouth as if about to reply but, in the silence, there was a crunch of stone from the far side of the cavern. Sophie turned, and saw a small shower of pebbles rolling down from a high ledge. In the shadows, something was moving.

Suddenly, a wild voice shrieked: 'Ha! As if a *child* like that could hurt us!'

Angelica! Sophie thought.

There was a huge gasp from the witch hunters. They turned, craning their necks to look up at the ledge. Angelica emerged, grinning, on the ledge above the witch hunters' heads. Clutched in her hands was the *Magic Most Dark* spell book. Her eyes gleamed, her pupils large and manic.

For a second of shocked, absolute silence, all the

witch hunters stared up at her. Then there was uproar.

'Witch!'

'Catch her!'

'Demagick her!'

The witch hunters rushed for their equipment. Sophie saw a man throw open his suit jacket to reveal rows of test tubes. A group of women began to chant frantically. Elvira Carver put her hands in her pockets and pulled out handfuls of shimmering, poisonous-looking green dust.

Angelica laughed as she looked down at them. 'Don't bother!' she yelled. She held *Magic Most Dark* above her head, the candlelight gleaming on its bronze clasps. 'We've outwitted you, Robert and I. We have created a book of spells, combining witch and witch hunter magic, and it's stronger than either alone!'

She stepped aside and out of the shadows came Robert Lloyd. He looked exhausted, but his face was firm with determination.

There was another gasp from the witch hunters.

'The traitor!'

Sophie heard the mutter go around the cavern. The witch hunters closest to her snarled openly, and the crowd surged towards Angelica and Robert.

Sophie pulled back, her heart beating fast, straining to see into the darkness behind the two outcasts. *Dad, where are you?*

Katy held her head in her hands. 'Robert must be crazy,' she said desperately. 'They'll kill him. Nothing matters to witch hunters more than loyalty! They hate traitors even more than they do witches!' She turned away, trembling. 'I can't watch this.'

Callum put his arm around her. 'Can't we do something? It looks like a fight's going to kick off!' he said.

Mr Gibson stepped forward from the crowd, scowling. 'You! Robert Lloyd! How dare you show your face here? You have betrayed your family, betrayed your calling—'

'I love Angelica!' Robert shouted back. He looked around at the witch hunters. Sophie could see he was breathing fast, like a trapped animal. 'I don't care if she's a witch. We only want to be left alone.'

Mr Gibson laughed, and the witch hunters echoed him.

'Wait, hear me out!' Robert went on. 'I know better than to appeal to your pity. So I have a proposal – one I think you won't be able to resist.'

The witch hunters muttered, looking at each other doubtfully.

Robert reached behind him into the shadows, and pulled something forwards. Sophie stifled a cry as she saw it was her father. He was still frozen, his face still in the same expression of shock that it had worn when he was trapped.

'Whoa! Is that your—' Callum burst out, turning to Sophie. Thankfully his voice was drowned by the collective gasp from the witch hunters.

Robert held Franklin by the shoulders. 'Here is Franklin Poulter, the most wanted witch. If you agree to leave Angelica and me alone, you can have him. And do what you want with him.'

Sophie began to tremble.

There was a moment's silence, and then the Master spoke. 'A very interesting proposal.' He stared at Franklin, stroking his chin thoughtfully. 'We have pursued Franklin Poulter for many, many years,' he said. 'I think we must agree to your proposal. Friends?'

Robert looked at the witch hunters. 'You swear on your honour to let me and Angelica go safely? You won't hunt us any more?'

There was a second's silence, and then a roar of assent from the witch hunters.

Robert's face flushed with relief. 'Here he is then – take him!' He held his hands above Franklin's wrists, scattering a pinch of dark powder over his wrists, crying out: 'Stone, shatter!'

Sophie's dad gasped and his hands flew up, free; but before he could do anything, Robert pushed him over the ledge. The witch hunters surged forwards to catch him, Mr Gibson tearing her father's pocket watch, his Source, from his shirt front.

Sophie swayed. They were going to demagick her dad, maybe even kill him. 'Dad!' She tried to run towards him, but Callum caught her arm.

'Sophie, no!'

'Let me go! I have to help him!' Sophie struggled against his grip.

'They'll kill you!' Katy sobbed.

Nothing mattered but saving her father. Sophie wrenched her arm free and ran into the cavern. Katy tried to follow but Callum held her back.

'*Let him go!*' Sophie screamed.

SEVENTEEN

The witch hunters swung round to stare at Sophie. She didn't care. She pushed through the crowd towards her father, but a wall of frowning witch hunters blocked her way. Among them was Mrs Gibson, her mouth round with shock.

'Sophie!' she exclaimed, and her faced flushed. 'What are you doing here?'

'I've come to save my dad,' Sophie said, trembling.

'You ... your ... wait! You mean, Franklin Poulter is your *father*?' Mrs Gibson paled, and she swung round to look at Franklin, then back to Sophie. 'But he's a witch!' Her face turned even paler when she looked behind Sophie. '*Katy!* What are *you* doing here?'

Sophie turned to see that Katy had followed her.

'I've come to help my friend.' Katy's voice shook.

'But ... I don't understand. She says her father's a witch!'

Katy looked at Sophie.

'Yes, he is,' Sophie said, then swallowed hard. 'And so am I!'

'But you've been to our house!' Mrs Gibson looked disgusted, as if she had trodden in something. 'You're our daughter's best friend!' She looked as if she were about to faint.

In the shocked silence, Katy moved to stand next to Sophie. Sophie could feel her shaking.

'Katy, how long have you known?' Mr Gibson demanded.

Katy gulped. 'Ages,' she said. Her voice steadied as she went on. 'And I agree with Robert. I'm friends with Sophie no matter if she's a witch or not. I'll never betray that.'

'But you'd betray your own family?' Mrs Gibson asked bitterly.

Katy looked stricken. 'Mum, I—'

'You don't understand,' Sophie broke in, turning to look around at the witch hunters. 'You hate witches just because they're witches, but we're just like you – some of us are good and some are bad. We could work together for common goals, we could use our powers for good, not to harm people—'

She was interrupted by a roar of scornful laughter.

'How dare you!' One of the witch hunters, a fat woman in a flowery dress, stepped forwards, her chins trembling indignantly. 'As if we are anything like witches!'

'Repulsive nonsense!' a man with a posh voice exclaimed, looking down his nose at Sophie.

'You silly little brat!'

Sophie started and looked up. The Master was pushing through the crowd, glaring at her with hatred. 'Did you really think we'd fall for a witch's pretty words?'

Sophie flinched at the venom in his voice. The man

looked up as Mr Gibson and the other witch hunters came pushing through the crowd, dragging Sophie's dad with them, his hands tied behind his back. Mr Gibson held his gold pocket watch triumphantly. Behind them came Robert and Angelica. The crowd parted around them, and then closed up behind them.

The Master of the Witch Hunt stepped forwards and smiled as he gazed into Franklin's face. Sophie moved closer, but Katy caught her hand, giving her a warning glance.

'At last,' the Master murmured.

'We can go now?' Robert asked.

The Master looked up at him and smiled slowly. 'Oh, I don't think so.' He chuckled, and the other witch hunters joined in the laughter.

'Our bargain—' Robert began.

'We never bargain with traitors!' the Master roared, a vein threatening to pop in his temple. Quick as a snake striking, he grabbed Franklin and pushed him back into the crowd of witch hunters. 'We have Franklin, we have his Source, and we'll demagick him. But now there's nothing to stop us getting rid of you, too, is there?' He spun round to Sophie. 'Or you,' he hissed, his red-rimmed eyes boring into hers. 'Witches and witch hunters should *never* work together. The very idea is an abomination! It is time for you to die.'

Sophie was paralysed with fear, but then she heard a voice shout, 'Not if I've got anything to do with it!'

She looked up. Callum had climbed up to the ledge where Angelica had been standing and was leaning against a boulder that was precariously placed on the edge. He pushed the boulder forwards. It teetered; then fell.

The boulder thundered towards them, bringing smaller stones with it. The Master took one look at the avalanche heading for him, and ran. The other witch hunters hastily scattered as the boulder, missing Sophie's father by inches, smashed into the wall close by them.

As the dust cleared, Sophie ran towards her dad.

'Sophie, are you OK?' he asked, taking her face in his hands.

'Fine, Dad. Are you?'

'They took my Source – my Source!' he gasped.

Katy and Callum were by her side. They grabbed fragments of the stone and together sawed through the ropes that bound his hands. Sophie's dad struggled free, but his face was full of agony.

'Run, Dad! We can't get it back now!' Sophie pulled him away, towards the tunnel that led back to the sea cave. 'We've got to escape.' Through the clouds of dust she could see that the witch hunters were already moving towards them again, Mr and Mrs Gibson at their head.

'Stop!' screamed a voice. It was Angelica.

She burst through the crowd. She was dragging someone with her and, as she swung to face them, Sophie saw it was Ashton. Angelica had his arm bent behind his back and her long nails dug into his throat. Robert was behind her, holding the book.

'Try to stop us, and I'll kill the boy!' Angelica hissed.

'No!' Mrs Gibson screamed.

'Please, don't hurt my son!' Mr Gibson cried out.

'Then let me through!' Dragging Ashton, they headed for the passage to the sea cave.

Sophie, Callum and Katy waited a second then

raced after them. The witch hunters, still shocked and confused, let them pass.

'Sophie, what are we going to do? She's got my brother!' Katy said as they ran. 'I don't know how to stop her!'

Sophie's mind worked fast. She only had one idea – but she hardly dared say it aloud. 'Do you know how to demagick a witch?'

Katy stopped moving. She looked shocked. 'I've never done it, but I know how to.'

Sophie took Katy by the shoulders. 'It's the only way,' she said, hardly believing her own words as they came out.

Katy looked at her, eyes wide. 'Are you sure?'

Sophie hesitated. It was a horrible idea. But Ashton's life was at stake. 'Yes.'

Katy struggled with her backpack. Test tubes and vials fell onto the ground and rolled here and there. She snatched them up. 'Phoenix tears, granite dust, ground fulgurite, mercury, condensed breath from a familiar ...' She tipped the ingredients one by one into a test tube, corked it and shook it. Purple vapour began to seep around the cork, and there was a strong smell of iron, like spilled blood, which grew stronger when Katy removed the stopper.

Sophie covered her mouth and nose. The smell made her want to be sick.

Ahead of them, Angelica turned suddenly, sniffing the air.

Katy lifted the test tube above her head. She hesitated for a second, glancing at Sophie. Sophie gulped and nodded. Callum looked on, his face pale with disbelief.

'Neither by dark nor light, day nor night, shall you ever again cast a spell, Angelica Poulter!' Katy cried.

Angelica stumbled to a halt. She turned towards them and, for the first time, Sophie saw real terror on her face.

The purple vapour bubbled out of the test tube and up to the roof of the cavern. From the purple clouds came rumbling, grumbling noises, like distant, angry voices.

Franklin ran up beside Sophie. 'What are you doing?' he cried out.

'There's no choice, Dad!' Sophie said.

'Wait! I'll—' He flung out his hands towards Angelica as if about to cast a spell, then stopped, a look of horrible realisation on his face as he remembered Mr Gibson had his Source.

'It's up to Katy now, Dad!' Sophie said to him. Katy had proved to her dad she'd been right before. He would have to trust her this time.

'. . . By the Thirteen Families I swear it.' Katy's arms shook, as if the test tube were heavy. 'By the moon and the sun I command it!' Sweat rolled down her face as more purple vapour belched out of the test tube and joined the clouds that were massing at the roof of the cave.

Callum gaped up at them.

'Come from her, magic!' Katy stretched out a hand, the other still holding the test tube.

Sophie looked towards Angelica. She didn't change. Nothing happened.

The terror had gone from Angelica's eyes and she laughed. 'Ha! As if *you* could demagick me!'

Katy's face fell as she looked at Sophie. 'I thought I did it right,' she began.

Ashton struggled, clawing Angelica's hand away from his throat. 'Katy! Witch blood!' he shouted. 'You need a drop of witch bl—' His voice choked off as Angelica snarled and covered his mouth with her hand.

Thinking quickly, Sophie snatched the Bloodhound from around Katy's neck and dug the needle deep into her own thumb. For a second there was no pain, and then she gasped as she felt it. A bead of blood welled up.

Sophie stared at it. There was still time to change her mind. But what about her grandmother, and Ashton?

Katy held the test tube in front of her, and Sophie squeezed her thumb hard so that a single drop of bright red blood splashed into the mixture.

The clouds above them rumbled. The ground shook. The mixture in the test tube bubbled, and boiled over so fast that in a couple of seconds Sophie couldn't see Katy any more. She heard her, though.

'By the moon and the sun I command it. Draw forth her powers!'

Angelica screamed. The clouds parted and, as they did so, Sophie saw Robert Lloyd. He was running towards them, rubbing a potion over his hands. As he drew nearer, an orb formed between his rubbing palms, growing and growing. It was golden, and fire burned inside it. Suddenly, he flung the orb at Katy. There was a flash like lightning and, before Sophie could react, she heard a thud. Then Katy screamed.

Through a break in the clouds around them, Sophie saw Katy lying on the floor, rolling in agony and clutching her leg. A glow of throbbing light surrounded her. The test tube had smashed onto the ground and the liquid was seeping away into the cracks in the rocks.

'Katy!' Callum screamed.

Sophie tried to run towards her, but she found herself pushed back. She realised that Robert's orb had contained a force field as well, stopping her from getting close to Katy. Then the purple clouds roiled in between her and Katy again, and Sophie couldn't see her.

Why hadn't the gold in Katy's bracelet worked to

protect her, she wondered desperately. Of course – Robert wasn't a witch. He was a witch hunter!

Behind them, the witch hunters were screaming and yelling in confusion, pointing at Robert.

'That's witch magic! He used witch magic!'

'It's impossible! He's a witch hunter!'

As the clouds drew back, Sophie looked down to see that Katy had gone. Turning fast, she saw Angelica and Robert running into the passage. Angelica was dragging Ashton after her, and Robert had a limp bundle tossed over his shoulder.

'Katy!' Callum yelled again.

Sophie's head spun. They had taken her best friend!

EIGHTEEN

Sophie turned to the witch hunters. 'They've taken Katy and Ashton!' she shouted. She looked at the witch hunters' blank faces and her voice rose to a scream that hit the roof of the cave. '*Help* us!'

But they didn't seem to be listening to her. Instead, they stared after Angelica. Horrified, terrified voices spoke up from the crowd.

'Did you see that?'

'That was a hybrid – witch and witch hunter powers together!'

'It can't be possible!'

'What are we going to do?'

'Retreat!'

'Kill them all!'

'We need to vote!'

Sophie covered her ears. 'Shut up!' she screamed. 'We can help you rescue them – my father and I – but we've got to be quick!'

The witch hunters stared at her as if she were a monster.

'Helped by a witch?' one said. 'This mixing of powers is evil!'

More uproar broke out. Sophie shook her head in despair. It would need the power of both witches and witch hunters to defeat Angelica and Robert's combined magic. She turned and ran towards the passage, not knowing what she would do.

She'd only gone a few paces when a voice shouted, 'Stop! Wait! Let us join you!'

The crowd fell silent in surprise. As Sophie turned back, she saw Mr Gibson pushing through the crowd. His wife came after him.

'Please!' Mr Gibson grabbed Sophie's arm but Sophie shook him off. 'Let us help, they've taken our children. Please!'

Sophie wasn't sure what to think.

There was a rumble of angry voices from the crowd, and someone at the back shouted: 'Traitors!'

Mrs Gibson turned towards the crowd, and shouted, 'But they've got our *children*!'

Sophie decided to trust them. 'Come on!' she said. She turned and raced into the passage. Mr and Mrs Gibson followed.

Sophie burst out of the end of the passage and skidded to a halt just behind her dad and Callum. She saw they were too late. Robert stood tall in the speedboat, which he was steering towards the cave exit. At a glance Sophie saw that Angelica was in the boat too, and so were Katy and Ashton. Angelica was tying their hands tightly.

'Stop!' Sophie and Callum screamed together.

'Let them go, Angelica,' Sophie's dad shouted over the noise of the engine. 'They're only children. What harm can they do?'

Angelica let out a wild cackle. 'None. But I can harm them, all right.'

'I'm not going to let you,' Sophie's dad growled. He raised his hands, but his face fell as again he realised his Source was missing. Angelica laughed, and the boat pulled away towards the open sea.

Sophie looked back as Mr and Mrs Gibson came running into the cave.

'Please don't do this!' Mrs Gibson yelled out across the water.

Mr Gibson charged into the water towards the boat. 'Robert,' he cried, wading forwards, 'please, stop! Ashton and Katy are your family, your own blood – you can't hurt them!'

Robert laughed a hard laugh over his shoulder and slowed the boat momentarily. 'What family? You cast me out, remember?' He smiled at his wife. 'Angelica is my family.'

The motorboat roared away, out of the cave and into the night, the sound of the motor dying away in the distance.

'The dinghy – quick – we've got to follow them!' Mr

Gibson ran for the boat and leaped in, the others following closely behind him. Callum reached for the oars and Mr Gibson joined him.

Sophie's dad hoisted the sail as they left the shelter of the cave. The wind whipped out the canvas and they sped over the sea in the wake of the motorboat. But the motorboat was way ahead of them.

'They're too fast! We'll never catch them,' Callum cried.

'Franklin – here.' Mr Gibson held something out that gleamed in the light. Sophie saw that it was her father's Source.

'Take it! Save our children, please!' Mrs Gibson was half sobbing.

Sophie's father snatched his watch back with a look of gratitude. He stood up in the boat, the wind blowing his dark coat backwards, the watch swinging from its chain.

'Earth, water, wind and fire – lend us all your speed!' he cried aloud.

The wind suddenly picked up, and Callum gasped as the mainsail rope was nearly jerked from his hands. The sea trembled and shook.

'It's an earthquake!' Mrs Gibson exclaimed.

'Just a little one,' Sophie's dad said brusquely, his brow furrowed with concentration.

Sophie turned to see a dark wave rising behind them, coming towards them fast. 'Dad . . . ' she began.

'Don't be afraid!' he replied.

The wave and the wind caught them at the same moment, and Sophie's words were blown back in her mouth as the boat leaped forwards. Salt spray stung her eyes and the wind hummed in the sail. Callum and Mr Gibson hung onto it to keep it under control as the boat zoomed forwards, carried on the crest of the tsunami and forced forwards by the wind. Sophie, squinting against the wind, saw Robert's horrified face looking back at them, and caught his words as they approached the motorboat.

'. . . let them go! We've got to escape!'

Angelica turned to face the dinghy, looking furious. She came towards them, pushing Katy ahead of her. At first Sophie didn't realise what she meant to do, but then Angelica forced Katy up onto the edge of the boat. Katy moved clumsily, her leg still clearly hurting and her hands tied behind her. In a moment of sick horror, Sophie realised what was about to happen.

'You want your children? Here they are!' Angelica shouted. Robert also came forwards, pushing Ashton, who also still had his hands bound.

'No!' Mrs Gibson screamed.

Sophie's dad brought his hands down hard, and the wave flattened and disappeared, leaving them sailing just behind the motorboat. Katy teetered on the edge of the boat.

How could she save them? Sophie looked up. The purple clouds from the demagicking ritual had been drawn down the passage and out of the sea cave, and were now building around the island in a thunderhead-shaped cloud. Maybe, if she finished the ritual, the demagicking could still work!

She tried to think back, to remember the words Katy had used for the demagicking ritual. Raising her hands, she began to chant.

'Neither by dark nor light,' Sophie started. Angelica gasped and froze. 'Day nor night' – the purple clouds rumbled and began to grow – 'shall you ever again cast a spell.' Sophie looked into her aunt's eyes and again saw the terror there. 'Angelica Poulter!'

The sea around the dinghy began to bubble. The bubbles multiplied, as if the sea were boiling, and they drifted towards Angelica. The purple clouds billowed towards them, covering over the sky.

'Draw forth her powers!' Sophie went on.

'Sophie?' her father shouted. 'What are you doing? That's witch hunter magic!'

Sophie gulped. She knew she was doing the worst thing in the world that could be done to a witch. Did Angelica deserve it? Would her father ever forgive her? But she had no choice. She couldn't let Katy die.

'I'm sorry, Dad!' Sophie shouted back.

She lifted her hands into the air, trying to remember the last words that Katy had said. Except ... *I don't know how it ends!* she thought in horror. Her mind was blank. Angelica was holding Katy out over the water, about to tip her in. Sophie was going to fail, Angelica would get away, and Katy would die.

'Sophie!'

Sophie turned as she heard Mr and Mrs Gibson shouting to her.

'It has to be you who finishes the incantation now you've begun it! Repeat after me,' Mr Gibson said. '*By the Thirteen Families I swear it. By the moon and the sun I command it.*'

Sophie licked her lips and frowned in concentration. 'By the Thirteen Families I swear it.' She took a deep breath. 'By the moon and the sun I command it,' she echoed.

The clouds bubbled and billowed. Grey smoke rose from the seawater, coiling and curling upwards. When it touched the purple clouds they, too, turned grey.

'Now say, "*Draw forth her powers*",' Mr Gibson shouted. 'And say it twice.'

'Draw forth her powers,' Sophie said.

Angelica shuddered and howled as the clouds descended on her.

Sophie shivered with horror. At last, she whispered, 'D-draw forth her powers.'

A vapour rose from Angelica's body, green as her

hair slide. It mingled with the grey clouds, like strands of silk twisting together.

Sophie looked up into the roiling clouds and flinched. She seemed to see shapes inside them: ancient faces and grinning mouths; long fingers twirling around the green vapour, winding it up and away from Angelica. There was a final rumble, and a flash of green lightning in the grey mists.

Angelica staggered, pulling Katy with her. To Sophie's horror, both of them fell over the edge of the boat, splashing into the water like stones.

'Angelica!' Robert screamed. He let go of Ashton and reached for the spell book, riffling his way frantically through the pages. But instead of running away, Ashton charged straight at Robert, his head down. He cannoned into him with such force that he knocked the book from Robert's hands. It flew into the air and landed in the water.

Robert gasped, winded, and fell to the floor of the boat. Ashton, unable to stop himself, teetered on the edge and hit the water a second after the book.

At the same time, Sophie's dad had gasped: 'My

sister!' He had flung himself into the sea, and Sophie saw him swimming towards Angelica.

Katy's parents leapt into the water too, and, without thinking, Sophie jumped in after them. Cold, salty darkness roared up in her ears as she struck out, feeling here and there with her hands, looking for her best friend. She wouldn't be able to bear it if she lost her.

She couldn't imagine what would happen if Katy died.

NINETEEN

The pressure of the water pushed down on Sophie as she flailed her arms. It was deep and cold, and she felt nothing.

I have to find Katy, she pleaded to herself. If only there was some magic that could help.

Then Sophie's fingers brushed something and she grasped it. It was a hand: Sophie's heart rose. Desperate for oxygen, she struck for the surface, pulling the person with her.

Sophie burst out of the water, gasping for breath.

Her lungs burned, and her legs and arms ached. She looked around, but it wasn't Katy she had dragged with her: it was Ashton.

His face was white and his eyes were shut. Sophie supported his head and began to swim backwards towards the shore, pulling him with her, all the while looking frantically for Katy. When she saw Mr Gibson, soaked and shivering, stumbling out of the sea with Katy in his arms, a cry of relief escaped her lips.

Mrs Gibson waded into the water to help her as she drew near the beach.

'Oh, thank you, Sophie, thank you!' She pulled Ashton from her and half carried, half dragged him onto land. Sophie staggered after them, her lungs still painful.

'Katy?' she gasped, and she ran to her best friend's side.

'She's alive.' Tears rolled down Mr Gibson's face as he gently cradled his daughter's head.

Sophie kneeled and leaned over Katy. Katy blinked and smiled up at her. 'You saved my life ... again!' she whispered, her voice rasping.

'Hey, what are friends for?' Sophie grinned at her, holding back her tears of relief. Next to her, Ashton choked and coughed as he came back to consciousness. Sophie smiled over at him. She was so happy to have saved him. But that was natural, right?

Sophie took Katy's hand and they sat like that for a few minutes, both of them recovering, and calming their thoughts. Then Katy clutched her arm. Sophie followed her gaze towards Callum, who was sitting, looking exhausted, on the sand.

'Sophie, I've ruined it,' Katy whispered miserably. 'He hates me now. I knew he would. How could anyone want to go out with me now they've seen how witch hunters act?'

'Don't say that!' Sophie hugged her tightly. 'Callum's better than that. You're not like them – you're you.'

'Robert has escaped,' her father said grimly. Sophie looked up. Her father knelt on the ground, holding Angelica in his arms. Her straggly, wet hair was plastered to her skull and her face was very pale. She wasn't moving.

Sophie scrambled across the stones and dropped

down by her dad's side. Angelica's eyes were open but unseeing, her face tinged with blue. 'Is she ... is she ...'

'No, she's not dead,' her father broke in. He stroked the hair back gently from Angelica's face. 'It was the demagicking. It sometimes leaves witches catatonic like this.'

Sophie put a hand to her mouth. 'Oh, Dad, I didn't mean to hurt her—' she began.

'Don't you dare feel guilty,' her father interrupted her. He put an arm around her shoulder and hugged her fiercely. 'You saved us all with your quick thinking. I always said I would do whatever was necessary to protect my family. But you really did it. You are a very brave girl, and I'm proud of you.'

'Hear, hear!'

Sophie turned, surprised at the warmth in Mr Gibson's voice. She blushed as she saw him and Mrs Gibson smiling at her. Mr Gibson had his arm around Katy and Mrs Gibson was holding Ashton, who was pale and shaking, but very much alive.

Sophie's dad jumped to his feet. 'What am I thinking?

You're all soaking, and cold.' He hunted around the beach, and came back with a piece of driftwood. He rubbed it hard, and it burst into flames. Holding the piece of wood up, he blew at it and Sophie gasped as the flame came away from the branch and floated towards her. She flinched as it touched her, but instead of burning, she felt as warm as if she were sitting next to a radiator. Steam rose around her as her clothes dried.

The flame grew and grew, like a bubble, until it enveloped all of the people on the beach. Angelica's hair crinkled up again into wild curls.

Mr Gibson turned to Sophie's dad. 'We can't thank you enough,' he said. 'Without you and Sophie, we would have lost our children.' He shook his head. 'I still can't quite grasp it. That a witch could use witch hunter magic ... '

'Perhaps we're more similar than we think,' Sophie's dad said.

Mr Gibson held out his hand and Sophie's dad shook it. Their eyes met, and though they did not smile, Sophie could tell that something had changed between them – for the better.

'We will do whatever we can to promote peace between witches and witch hunters,' Mr Gibson said. 'But I can't promise you it will be easy.'

Sophie's father nodded. 'I'll do the same within the witch community. And you're right; it won't be easy. But we have to try.'

'The book's gone,' said Sophie blankly. She had only just realised what that meant. 'Dad, the book's gone, and neither Angelica nor Robert can help us. We won't be able to take the spell off Grandma now.' She couldn't hold back a sob.

Her father placed a hand on her shoulder.

'Let's cross that bridge when we come to it. First, we must get you three back to the campsite, or there will be a lot of explaining to do.'

'Oh, I don't think—' Mrs Gibson exclaimed, holding on to Katy protectively.

'We can't let our children go back there,' Mr Gibson finished. 'They should be at home after the shock they've had – and there's no reason, now, for them to be at Turlingham.'

'Dad!' Katy exclaimed in horror.

'What do you mean?' Mr Gibson looked puzzled. 'There's no reason for you to stay—'

'No reason for *you*, maybe,' Katy said firmly. 'I went to the school because you wanted me to, but now I want to stay there because *I* want to. Because I've got friends there.' She smiled at Sophie. 'Best friends.'

'Katy's right.' Sophie jumped as she realised it was Ashton who had spoken. He was pale but his green eyes were as keen as ever. 'It isn't fair to make us leave – and besides, it would look suspicious, don't you think?'

Mr and Mrs Gibson exchanged a worried look and then shrugged.

'Well, since you put it that way.' Mr Gibson nodded. The adults moved off, deep in conversation.

'Yes!' burst out Callum. Katy and Sophie looked at him in surprise. Callum blushed bright red. 'I mean, I'm really glad you're not leaving, Katy,' he added, in a lower voice.

Katy's face broke into smiles. 'You are? I mean . . . I thought you wouldn't like me any more.'

'What?' Callum looked puzzled. 'Katy, I'd like you

whatever you are – witch, witch hunter, or elf! I was just, well, a little . . . surprised.'

'Really?' Katy beamed.

'Of course!' Callum glanced around to check her parents weren't looking, then leaned over and kissed her.

Sophie hid a smile and turned away. It looked as if she was going to be a spare part for a while longer. But she didn't mind at all! If Katy and Callum could make things work, maybe there *was* hope for her mum and dad, after all.

They made their way slowly up the cliff path towards the campsite, her father supporting Angelica. Angelica seemed to be in a deep sleep.

'Is there a spell we can cast to make her better?' Sophie asked. She hated seeing her aunt like that; hated that it was she who'd caused it.

Her father smiled at her. 'Wasn't it you who said that love was the greatest magic of all? Angelica is my sister, and whatever she does, I will always love her. We'll look after her until she's well again.'

Sophie smiled back, relieved and happy.

'Sophie!'

Sophie turned around to see Ashton beckoning her back down the path. Her heart sank. What did he want with her now? What mean thing could he say to her after all this? But it wasn't as if he could tease her about being a witch, not when it was out in the open.

Reluctantly, she dropped behind the others to see what he wanted.

Ashton glanced towards his parents, then caught Sophie's hand and pulled her behind a boulder. Sophie's heart lurched, and she opened her mouth to scream for help – only to find Ashton kissing her.

Sophie was too shocked to move. Ashton's arms were around her, and it felt … good! She couldn't help herself, and kissed him back for a moment. Then, summoning up all her strength, she pushed him away.

'Are you crazy?' she burst out. 'Hello, Ashton? I'm a witch! You don't have to try and prove it any more – everyone knows.' She looked around for iron filings, or Bloodhounds, but there were none in sight.

'I know,' Ashton mumbled. To Sophie's surprise, he was blushing. 'I'm *not* trying to prove you're a witch!'

'Oh, come on.' Sophie folded her arms. 'You've been doing it all term.'

'You don't get it!' Ashton said. He ran a hand through his damp hair, making it stand up on end. 'Sophie, I didn't want to prove you were a witch. I wanted to prove you *weren't*!' He was red in the face. 'Because I . . . I like you a lot. Really, a lot. And it didn't make sense, because you were a witch. But, Sophie, I don't care about that any more.' His words came out in a rush. 'I don't care if you're a witch. I just want you to be my girlfriend.'

Sophie stared at him, open-mouthed. Ashton was blushing but she could tell that he was sincere. He was looking straight in her eyes. And he'd kissed her. 'You really don't care that I'm a witch?' she said. Her voice softened as she realised how much he must like her, to go against all his training and upbringing.

Ashton shook his head. 'You're Sophie. That's all I care about.'

Sophie opened and closed her mouth but no words

came out. Ashton's green eyes were fixed on her, and there was a look in them that she'd never seen before – it was both humble and desperate. For an instant her heart felt as sweet and warm as melting chocolate ... and then she remembered how he'd always been so mean to Katy, and how much he'd hurt her.

She stepped back. 'I'm glad you don't hate witches any more, and I'm flattered that you want to ask me out. But, Ashton, you've been horrible to me ever since I've known you.'

Ashton bit his lip. He looked ashamed.

'I don't care if you're a witch hunter, but ... ' Sophie took a deep breath. 'Ashton, I don't want to go out with someone like you.' She swallowed, seeing the look on Ashton's face. 'I'm sorry.'

Ashton hung his head. 'I can't blame you. I *have* been horrible, I know. I'm sorry. But I promise' – he looked up, his eyes alight – 'I promise I'll change. I'll prove I'm not the horrible person I seem to be.' He reached out his hands to her. 'Then will you go out with me?'

Sophie backed away, shaking her head. 'Ashton, no.'

His face fell. Trying not to have second thoughts,

Sophie turned and hurried to catch up with the others. It was the right thing to do, to turn Ashton down.

But because of the way her heart ached, at that moment it didn't feel quite like the right thing at all.

'Uh-oh,' Callum exclaimed as they came through the woods towards the campsite. 'Looks as if they've realised we were missing.'

In the dawn light, Sophie could see two police cars parked in the lane. Students stood around in huddled groups, looking frightened and serious. Maggie and Mr Powell were talking to a policeman.

Her father stopped dead, frowning.

'This is going to be difficult to explain to your mother,' he said, as if to himself.

'Mr Poulter?' It was Callum who spoke up, to Sophie's surprise. 'I think you should tell her the truth.' Sophie's father's eyebrows rose. 'Honestly,' Callum went on. 'I'm glad Katy finally told me. I'm glad she could trust me. Maybe . . . maybe you just have to trust Sophie's mum. If you want her to trust you, that is.'

'Sophie!'

236

Her mother's scream cut through the air. Sophie looked round to see her mother running towards her across the field, her arms out. Reaching them, she flung her arms around Sophie and squeezed her in a tight hug. 'Oh, Sophie! What happened? Where did you go? I've been so worried.'

Sophie's heart ached with guilt. 'Oh, Mum, I'm really sorry—' she began.

Her mother interrupted her as she saw her father. 'Franklin! Where did you come from? What are you doing with Sophie?' Her voice faltered as she saw Angelica. 'And who on earth is that woman? And . . .' She stared over her husband's shoulder. 'Mr and Mrs Gibson?' She stared blankly back and forth between them. 'I – I don't understand. Ashton? You were suspended! What are you all *doing* here?'

Sophie's father cleared his throat and glanced around at the others.

'Tamsin, I owe you an explanation.' He paused. 'The truth, this time.'

'The truth?' Sophie's mother gave a half-laugh. 'Well, I certainly hope so.'

'It *will* be the truth, Mum,' Sophie said.

Her father drew them away from the others, into the shelter of the trees.

'Tamsin,' he began in a low, serious voice. 'I have to tell you something.' He took a deep breath. 'Witches are real ...'

TWENTY

Sophie's grandma lay motionless in the bed. Around her, machines beeped and hummed. Her face was serene. Corvis – his wing in a splint – perched on the head of the bed, Gally sitting next to him. Sophie and her parents sat by the bed, Sophie's father looking calm and serious. Her mother locked her fingers together, nervously glancing between Corvis and Gally.

The door opened and Katy came in, looking breathless. 'Sorry I'm late. I had to skip Games to get here in time – oh, sorry, Mrs Morrow.' She blushed.

'That's OK, Katy. You can consider yourself excused this time.' Sophie's mum folded her arms tightly. 'I can't help thinking I must be the victim of a very cruel practical joke, though. I hope this . . . erm . . . spell of yours works.'

Katy and Sophie exchanged a glance. They hoped so, too. It was the first time they had ever tried to combine their magic and Sophie was nervous, even though they had spent so long planning.

'It will work,' said her father softly. 'Two are stronger than one, and Sophie and Katy have a bond like few others.'

Sophie and Katy locked eyes. Sophie took a deep breath and nodded. They stood on opposite sides of her grandmother's bed, Katy holding a glass bowl full of a liquid. It was as clear as water, but much thicker.

Sophie raised the sheet of paper she had been holding. It was the first time she had ever written a spell down, the first time that she hadn't just made up her chants on the spot. It was an odd feeling, as if she was working more like a witch hunter than a witch. Would it still work?

She took a deep breath and began to read:

'Earth, water, wind and fire. Give her the freedom she desires.'

Her finger tingled beneath her Source. Katy swirled the liquid in the bowl and added some drops of glittering powder to it. The liquid seemed to catch fire, burning with a flame that was almost invisible. Sophie's mother let out a small gasp, and Franklin squeezed her hand.

Sophie went on, gazing anxiously at her grandmother's face.

'Fire, water, wind and earth. Free her from the stony curse.'

Her grandmother's hand twitched suddenly. Sophie nearly shouted in excitement, but she forced herself to stay calm. Her finger felt as if it was halfway between freezing and burning now, and she felt the room grow strangely still, as if the whole of Nature was waiting for her next words.

Katy, her brow sweating, watched the flame as it burned on and on. The liquid slowly seemed to shrink in the bowl, as if it were evaporating.

'Water, earth, fire and wind. Show the thing that keeps her pinned.'

A feeling of power rushed through her, like being rolled in strong waves and Sophie shivered with a mixture of excitement and fear. Angelica had been right; mixing witch and witch hunter magic was much more powerful than using either one alone: it was like watching a big storm building on the horizon, and not knowing if it would sweep you away.

'Oh my goodness,' her mother said. 'What's that?'

She was pointing at a flickering shape around Sophie's grandmother's throat. But she clapped a hand over her mouth as, slowly, a stone necklace appeared. It lay around Sophie's grandmother's neck like a malevolent grey snake. Sophie shuddered.

The liquid in the bowl had almost all gone now: only a small, shimmering drop remained. Katy leaned over and blew the flame out.

'What do I do now?' she whispered to Sophie, anxiously.

'Just do what comes naturally, as if you were a witch.' Sophie smiled.

Katy licked her lips uncertainly. Then her brow cleared. She tipped the drop of remaining liquid very carefully from the bowl onto the necklace. There was a moment of silence as they all gazed anxiously at it.

For a second, Sophie was worried nothing would happen, and Katy's face fell. But then Sophie heard a sizzling noise, the drop of water seemed to smoke, and the stone necklace writhed. She gasped. The liquid was eating its way through the stone like acid. The necklace cracked in two and crumbled into dust.

'Fire, earth, wind and water. Be as strong as the love of her only granddaughter,' Sophie finished, tears welling up in her eyes. The necklace was gone, but would her grandmother wake up?

They gazed at her still form for a long moment.

Suddenly, unable to resist it, Sophie leaned down and kissed her grandmother on her cheek. 'Oh, please wake up, Grandma,' she whispered, feeling tears wet her eyelashes.

Her grandmother's eyelids flickered. A muscle at the corner of her mouth twitched. Her eyes opened slowly, and she smiled.

'Grandma!' Sophie shrieked, and she flung her arms around her. Her father was there a second later, and enveloped both of them in a huge hug.

'Mother, are you all right?' he asked.

'Better than all right!' Sophie's grandma laughed and pulled herself upright in the bed. 'That was extraordinary magic, Sophie and Katy. I've never felt anything quite like it.' She shook her head in wonder. Sophie hugged her again.

'Maybe it's because it was a spell of love,' she said. 'Oh, Grandma, it's so wonderful to have you back! We've got so much to tell you!'

'But not now—!' Sophie's dad broke in as the door opened and the doctor came rushing in, followed by some nurses.

'I heard the noise. Has there—' The doctor's mouth fell open as he saw Sophie's grandma smiling at him. 'What on earth . . .?'

Sophie stood back as the doctors and nurses descended on her grandmother. She grinned at Katy.

'We did it! Together!' They hugged each other tightly.

As they watched the nurses fussing over Sophie's grandma, Sophie's mum tugged at her husband's sleeve. She looked shell-shocked. 'That necklace,' she said. 'It came out of nowhere! And Loveday woke up ... So it really *is* all true. You're a ... and Katy is ... and Sophie, you're a ... '

Sophie nodded and exchanged a guilty, amused look with her father. 'Afraid so, Mum.'

'I see,' said Sophie's mother, distantly.

Her face went white.

'Uh-oh, not again!' Sophie's dad cried, as Sophie's mum fainted into his arms.

Watching her dad hold her mum, Sophie thought that things would be OK after all. Her weird, half-magical family would be fine.

Witches, witch hunter and humans – none of it really mattered, as long as you had the people you loved.